"Would You Like Some Wine?"

Jason asked. He took two crystal wine glasses from a small basket, poured the wine and offered her one of the goblets.

"You think of everything," Lila said, smiling and taking the glass from him. "This is simply wonderful." Jason moved closer to her and immediately her body became tense.

"I don't bite," he said, caressing her face slowly with his free hand.

"Of course you don't," Lila said nervously, "but I prefer that you not do that."

"Would you prefer that I do this?" His kiss was gentle and warm and Lila found herself responding to his embrace.

BARBARA SOUTH
has lived and traveled throughout Europe and the Caribbean. She now makes her home in Houston, Texas. This is her first Silhouette Romance.

Dear Reader:

Silhouette Romances is an exciting new publishing venture. We will be presenting the very finest writers of contemporary romantic fiction as well as outstanding new talent in this field. It is our hope that our stories, our heroes and our heroines will give you, the reader, all you want from romantic fiction.

Also, *you* play an important part in our future plans for Silhouette Romances. We welcome any suggestions or comments on our books and I invite you to write to us at the address below.

So, enjoy this book and all the wonderful romances from Silhouette. They're for *you!*

Karen Solem
Editor-in-Chief
Silhouette Books
P.O. Box 769
New York, N.Y. 10019

BARBARA SOUTH
Wayward Lover

Silhouette *Romance*

Published by Silhouette Books New York

America's Publisher of Contemporary Romance

SILHOUETTE BOOKS, a Simon & Schuster Division of
GULF & WESTERN CORPORATION
1230 Avenue of the Americas, New York, N.Y. 10020

Distributed by Pocket Books

ISBN: 0-671-57111-7

First Silhouette Books printing October, 1981

10 9 8 7 6 5 4 3 2 1

America's Publisher of Contemporary Romance

Printed in the U.S.A.

Thanks
Valerie and Vivian

Chapter One

Lila Drake swung her yellow MG convertible onto Westheimer Road and silently thanked her guardian angel for her recent good fortune. She was happier now than she ever dreamed possible. The financial investments her parents made for her ten years ago had finally paid off, giving her the opportunity to quit a job that had lost its challenge and to move from a city she no longer enjoyed. She had even found the courage to break off with Carl, her fiancé, who had become so jealous in the last few months she had almost given up her life-long dream of becoming a novelist. But just when she had begun to doubt herself most and give in to his insipid nagging demands, her luck changed. Bessit Publishing Company had shown interest in her book and if rewrites went well, she would soon be published. Her life was finally falling into place. Patience—the key to success.

Her drive took her east past the Galleria Shopping Center and under the 610 loop. A smile shaped her lips as she thought of the latest twist her life had taken. Fate had surely sent her to Houston to visit her only living relative Aunt Margaret, for after three days she had decided to stay. The city felt so right. She eagerly looked forward to sharing her life with the seventy-five year old woman who had just driven off a few minutes earlier to shop for swimsuits for a weekend holiday on South Padre Island. Aunt Margaret Drake was incredible.

Summer in Houston meant occasional semi-tropical weather and Lila became aware of the heat and humidity as she drove. She was glad she had pulled her thick auburn hair up in a pony tail and braided it. Her white cotton T-shirt and skirt were just right for the climate and she hoped not too casual for the occasion. Luckily the thin-strapped, white high-heeled sandals were the touch she needed to give her just a hint of elegance. She was convinced she had made the right choice of not wearing hose and hoped their absence wouldn't offend her Aunt Margaret's friends. Bless Aunt Margaret. She had been so concerned about her friends' grandnieces that she had practically begged Lila to help them. At first Lila had resisted, but later changed her mind. Although her finances were still on solid grounds she had given herself several treats—too much traveling and shopping in foreign countries. The generous pay that this job offered for a couple of hours two or three days a week would certainly help her to maintain her financial security and provide the freedom she needed to work on her book. Additionally, she felt she would enjoy the little girls and tutoring them would be a welcomed change of pace from her writing.

As she drove, Lila noted the many interesting shops and restaurants along the way. Houston had certainly grown since her last visit. She decided to stop and browse through one of the shops as soon as she spotted one that interested her, since she had time to spare before meeting her aunt's friends. She drove along singing softly to herself while the strong Texas sun lazily browned her naturally fair complexion. She began to speed up to make a light and thought better of it, bringing the MG to a smooth stop. As she waited for the light to change, she spied an antique shop across the street and decided to take a look inside, pulling into one of the parking spots provided for customers in front of the building.

The shop was divided into several rooms. Lila was told by a shop girl that the elegant, more expensive items were in the front rooms while the bargains had been placed in the back. She decided to initiate her browsing in the back rooms and work her way forward. She examined white iron beds, hat stands, candelabras, fireplace fixtures and old clocks. She especially liked a small brass clock that had been imported from France. She lingered over it for quite some time before deciding she could not afford another treat before earning another paycheck. She slowly made her way up to the front rooms inspecting exquisite grandfather and grandmother clocks, barometers, marble-top washstands and eighteenth- and nineteenth-century European tables, sofas, porcelains and fine silver. "This is a marvelous shop," she said to the shop girl when she finally arrived in one of the front rooms. "It must be loads of fun working here."

"I like it very much," the girl answered. Lila continued her browsing, picking up small objects here and there and thoroughly admiring larger more expensive ones.

"I knew I recognized that voice," Lila heard someone say behind her, "and I'm glad I came over to find its owner."

Lila turned around casually brushing stray strands of hair from her face. "Hunter Matthews!" she said and embraced her dearest friend of college days.

"Lila Drake! What are you doing here?" Hunter asked. "When did you get back? Tell me where you've been and what you've been doing," he said holding her by her slender shoulders.

Lila was so surprised to see her old friend that she was at a loss for words. "There's so much to tell," she finally said, not knowing where to begin.

"Come, let me buy you a drink." He took her by the arm and guided her out of the shop and across the street to Pepe's Mexican Restaurant. "Do you like Mexican food?"

"Love it."

They entered the gaily decorated establishment and were led to a table in front of a huge window. "We might as well have lunch," Hunter said, handing a menu to Lila.

"I'm too excited to eat much of anything," she said happily, "perhaps I'll just have a guacomole salad and a large iced tea."

"Sounds perfect," said Hunter, "I'll have the same." The waiter took their order and was back within a couple of minutes. They began eating the perfectly spiced salads and the warm corn chips that accompanied them. "Now tell me everything, Lila. Do you realize it's been six years?" he asked, looking at her intently.

"Yes, it has been a long time Hunter, and it's a real treat seeing you again." Lila excitedly sipped her iced tea.

"So what are you doing here?" he continued to question her.

"So I've moved back to Houston," she said mocking him playfully.

"To stay?"

"Yes to stay," she said feeling even more positive now about her decision to move back to Houston than she had ever felt before.

"I know you went to New York after graduation," he said. "Have you been there all this time?"

There was silence for a few moments as Lila remembered the many hours she and Hunter had shared dreaming of living in eastern American cities and traveling to foreign countries.

"I lived in New York only four years," she said

hesitantly, "then I moved to Boston and was there two years."

"Those are two of my favorite cities."

"I know. I've thought of you often during the past six years."

"Did you ever go abroad?" Momentarily, Lila felt a little guilty for she could see from the expression on Hunter's face that he had done none of the things they had dreamed about so long ago.

"I've been to many of the places we used to talk about so much, Hunter," she said. "I've seen Big Ben in London; the parks and gardens around Stuttgart in southwestern Germany; the Chateaux Country of France, Paris and several other cities of Europe. I've even managed to travel throughout Canada and the Carribean."

Again silence punctuated their conversation. "Sounds exciting," Hunter said finally. "Your travels have been extensive."

"Yes, it has been an exciting and rewarding time," she replied, "however, five years ago my parents were killed in a car accident in west Texas." She fought the memory of her parents' death. "That was the saddest day of my life," she added.

"Yes, I know." Hunter's mood had become warm and compassionate. "I was in Mexico on my honeymoon at the time. But I heard about the accident when I got back to Houston and tried to contact you to no avail, of course. I even tried to call Aunt Margaret, but she had an unlisted number. I'm sorry about your parents."

"Thank you. It's wonderful to know you remember Aunt Margaret," she said changing the subject to a happier one.

"Of course I remember her," Hunter said. His mood became lighter as he finished his salad and pushed his plate aside. "She's always been one of my favorite people. I still haven't found anyone who can top that chile of hers."

"Oh, she'll be so pleased to know you remember. I'm living with her until I find a place of my own. Why don't you and your wife come over for dinner one evening. By the way, who did you marry, Hunter? Do I know her?"

Hunter became pensive and he spoke softly. "No. You don't know her, Lila," he said. "Her name is Sarah Bell and she's from Utah. We're separated. But I'd love to come for dinner."

"I'm so sorry," Lila said, regretting she had caused his mood to pendulate again.

He took a deep breath and released it slowly. "That's the way it goes sometimes," he responded.

Once more Lila felt compelled to change the subject. "I'll ask Aunt Margaret about a time and let you know about dinner. May I call you?"

Hunter wrinkled his brow. "No doubt it would be more convenient if I call you," he replied. "I seem to spend most of my time away from a phone."

"Fine." She ate the last mouthful of her salad and washed it down with the iced tea.

"Now, why isn't a beautiful girl like you married?" Hunter began his probing again. "Are the men in New York and all those other places you've been to against marriage or something?"

Lila laughed lightly. She had never had the question put to her that way before. "No, I guess maybe I am," she said confidently. "I was engaged, Hunter, but decided he wasn't the right guy for me. I called it off. It was a wise decision. I know that now."

"So you're one of those liberated women who doesn't need a man," he said teasingly.

"No, not at all," Lila replied. "I just refuse to allow myself to be pressured into something because society says it's time. I'm twenty-seven and very capable of taking care of myself. I'm interested in writing books and have been told I have a promising future in the field. If love and marriage happens, it happens. If not, *c'est la vie*. The important thing is I'm happy with my life."

Hunter seemed deep in thought as he spoke. "I guess living in all those places and traveling helped you to develop that kind of philosophy," he said.

Lila looked at him and saw unhappiness in his gray eyes. She knew she had been extremely lucky. "I don't know if traveling has had any part in it's development," she said, "but I do know that for me it's the healthiest attitude to embrace."

Hunter shifted his long, lanky body in his seat and ran his thin pale fingers through his black hair. "That's good," he said. "I'm glad to see you so happy, Lila. So where were you going when I bumped into you?"

Lila was relieved the pendulum had once again swung to a lighter subject. "I'm on my way to meet some of Aunt Margaret's friends. They'd like me to do some tutoring for them."

"Oh yes," Hunter said, "someone told me you

had earned a Doctor of Education degree while you were in New York. Who and what will you tutor?"

"It was a Master of Education degree in Boston," she said. They both laughed at the misinformation. "I'll tutor two little girls in math and reading."

"That should be rewarding," said Hunter. "Good luck."

"Thank you." She glanced at the decorative clock on the wall. "Look at the time. It's hard to believe we've been here for more than an hour."

"It's been fun, Lila," Hunter said, "like old times. But I'd best be on my way." He got up from the table. "How do I contact you?" he asked.

"I'll give you Aunt Margaret's address and telephone number," she paused to jot them on a piece of paper. "If you don't call," she said handing the paper to him, "I'll be terribly disappointed." They left the table and walked toward the cashier. "Incidentally, is your law office still on San Jacinto?" Lila asked.

"Yes. I'm still there." He paid the bill and they left the restaurant.

"You're doing well?"

"I have no complaints." They crossed the street and walked to the parked cars. He opened the door to the MG and Lila slid under the wheel.

"Good luck again with your tutoring and your writing," he said. "You'll hear from me soon."

"Thanks. I'm looking forward to seeing you again." She started the car and pulled into the flow of traffic. Lady Luck was certainly holding out. Seeing Hunter again after so many years was an unexpected bonus in her day. She hoped they would be as good friends now as they had been in college. However, she realized that time and experiences do change people. She would just have to wait and see how things turned out. Nevertheless, it was sad about his marriage.

It's two o'clock, she said to herself after taking a quick glance at her watch, *I'd better hurry or I'll be late.*

She was now on Elgin Road looking for Caroline Street. She spotted it just a few yards ahead and changed lanes to make a right turn. As she pulled around the corner on the red light, which is legal in Texas, a maroon Mercedes Benz making a left onto Caroline Street barely missed her, and frightened Lila so that she pulled over, resting her head on the steering wheel. The driver in the Mercedes drove ahead of her, stopped his car and watched her in his rearview mirror. After a moment, he got out and walked over to the MG.

"Are you all right?" his deep voice demanded.

"I'm okay," she whispered, her head still resting on the steering wheel.

"Didn't you see me?" he asked angrily.

Lila raised her head and was taken aback by the strikingly handsome figure standing over her. His expensive suit was perfectly tailored for his tall lean form and the pale blue shirt he wore enhanced both his tanned complexion and the contemptuous expression that he wore on his face. "I didn't see you," was all she was able to say.

"I certainly hope starting now you'll make a habit of looking where you're going Miss," he snapped and strode back to his car. He sped away leaving Lila alone to regain her composure. When she became calm again she took a look at the number on the card that her Aunt Margaret had given her. The house she was looking for was right up the street. She drove slowly and carefully finally stopping in front of it. The turn-of-the-century mansion, which sat majestically amid giant oak trees, had at least fifteen rooms, plenty of windows and a large porch. For a moment she admired its architecture.

Lila checked her make up in her rear-view mirror, straightened the many gold chains she always wore around her neck and got out of the car. She went up several stone steps leading from the curb and walked the long sidewalk to more steps that led onto the porch. She pressed the button next to the heavy dark wooden door and waited. A few minutes elapsed before the door swung open and a cheery faced gray haired women of about seventy greeted her.

"You're Lila Drake," she said opening the door wide.

"Yes I am," Lila replied.

"I'd know Margaret's niece anywhere," the woman said. "I'm Katherine Tobias. Come in."

"Oh, you're Ms. Katherine," Lila said entering the house, "my aunt talks about you all the time. It's a pleasure to meet you."

"Thank you. It's a joy meeting you," Ms. Katherine said warmly. She led Lila through an elegant entry hall past a highly polished carved staircase into what was obviously a library. "Make yourself comfortable," she said gesturing for Lila to sit down.

Lila settled herself on the sofa feeling relaxed and happy again. "Are you going to South Padre Island with Aunt Margaret and the other ladies?" she asked.

"Indeed I am," Katherine Tobias said smiling. "As a matter of fact, I've just completed my packing. I'm sure we'll have a grand time."

"I'm sure you will, too," Lila said, facinated by the woman's vivaciousness.

"Now, my dear, I must tell Jason you're here. Please excuse me." The tall graceful figure left the room moving with such vitality that Lila wondered if perhaps the water in Houston had been treated with something special to give its citizens, especially the ones over sixty-five, such gusto. She quietly vowed to drink eight glasses a day as she allowed her eyes to roam around the huge room. The floor-to-ceiling bookcases which lined one wall were chocked with books, and the opposite wall accommodated a variety of antique maps. The map arrangement was interrupted by several windows which were beautifully draped with navy and beige print fabric. Large plants were scattered throughout the area and a deep piled beige rug covered the floor. A huge mahogany desk and chair were at one end of the room and a wood-burning fireplace covered the opposite wall completely. A long navy suede sofa sat under the antique maps and several beige suede chairs were arranged in front of it and around the room. Lila walked over to a table that held framed pictures of what she supposed were photographs of the family. She picked one up to take a closer look.

"So, we meet again Ms. Lila Drake," the familiar voice came from across the room.

She looked up and her eyes locked with those of

the man in the maroon Mercedes. "You're Jason Tobias?" she asked surprised to see him standing there.

"I am," he replied arrogantly. Jason had changed into a pair of beige gabardine slacks, a white close-fitting cotton shirt and brown leather Italian sandals which he wore with no socks. His dark curly hair framed his ruggedly handsome face and he seemed even more attractive now than he had the first time Lila saw him just a few minutes earlier.

Her hands began to shake as she sat the picture back in its place and she silently reprimanded herself for allowing this man to intimidate her. "I've come to see you about tutoring the girls," she said, and immediately felt foolish because he obviously knew why she was there.

"I'm aware of that Ms. Drake. Please sit down." He gestured toward the sofa but Lila chose a chair instead. Ms. Katherine came back into the room carrying a tray of frosted drinks and small delicate cakes. Jason met his aunt mid-way into the room and took the tray from her, placing it on a table next to the sofa.

"Don't sit over there my dear, come sit next to me here on the sofa." Ms. Katherine patted the cushion next to her. "I have a lovely fruit drink here that I know you'll just adore." Lila walked back across the room aware of Jason's brown eyes scrutinizing her. He stood until she was seated then handed her a drink and one of the small cakes.

"This is Margaret Drake's niece, Jason. Isn't she lovely?" Her eyes fastened on the young woman. Lila nervously took a sip of her drink and a small bite of cake. She was uncomfortable with the acute attention she was receiving.

"Very," Jason responded still inspecting her from the tip of her head down to the ends of her expertly polished toes.

"We know all about you my dear," the woman continued. "Margaret is very proud of you."

Lila could feel Jason's eyes on her and tried desperately not to allow her eyes to again meet his. However, she glanced up in time to notice him reexamine the smooth skin of her long thin legs. She shifted in her seat, wishing she had worn hose, and tried to concentrate on what Ms. Katherine was saying.

"Margaret has told me of your adventures abroad and your exciting life in those eastern cities. What a lucky girl you are, Lila," the older woman said, her bright eyes shining.

"I'm not sure I've had adventures," Lila said, a little embarrassed, "but I do enjoy the northeast and traveling."

"We're so lucky you've consented to help us," said Ms. Katherine. "You're just the young woman we need."

"Is she?" asked Jason, his brown eyes narrowing.

It was evident to Lila that Jason did not feel as his aunt did—fortunate that she had consented to tutor his nieces. He obviously disliked her on sight, and his antagonistic attitude vividly conveyed his feelings.

"Jason had wanted to hire a retired schoolteacher," Ms. Katherine replied, feeling she owed Lila an explanation for her nephew's apparent hostility.

"He's afraid you'll become involved with your writing and your work with Violet and Daisy will be less than sufficient. However, I think the girls need a young woman like you to take an interest in them and I'm grateful to you for your time. I know you'll give us your best."

"I'll do all I can," Lila said, thinking at least one person in the room was on her side.

"Then it's settled," said Ms. Katherine. "Now tell us about your book, Lila. It's so exciting meeting a writer."

"Well, I'm not published yet," she said. "However, my book is a love story."

"Oh, I just adore love stories," gushed Ms. Katherine.

Jason casually lounged in one of the suede chairs. "Are you sure you have time for us?" he asked.

"Yes. I'm positive." Lila had become annoyed with Jason but remained serene.

Nevertheless, she sensed that he was greatly concerned about the children's education and was reluctant to entrust their learning to someone who was neither interested in their well-being nor cared about their academic achievement. "Why are you so willing to help us?" he persisted.

"First of all, Mr. Tobias," Lila said looking directly at him and speaking firmly. "I want to help your nieces because I enjoy working with children. I have had two years experience teaching youngsters their age and from what Aunt Margaret has told me about them I know I can succeed in what you want done over the summer. Secondly, I'm very much interested in the salary that has been quoted and I have no intention of collecting pay that I have not earnestly and honestly earned."

"I see," Jason mused, "then I guess it is settled." His dark eyes narrowed once more as he fixed them on her.

"Good," said Ms. Katherine. "Now, I must leave." She placed her glass and plate on the side table. "I have an appointment. You stay here and finish your talk with Jason, my dear. I'm looking forward to seeing you again soon." She kissed Lila and Jason and walked swiftly toward the door. "Don't wait dinner for me Jason," she said pausing, "I'm eating out this evening with Margaret and some of the others."

Lila felt herself tense, realizing she had been left alone with Jason and tried, but to no avail, to deny that she found his insolent manner threatening, vowing on the spot to harness the feelings of inadequacy that he aroused in her. She quickly stuffed the last of her cake in her mouth and emptied her glass as Jason rose from his chair and walked about the room impatiently.

"I don't know how much your aunt has told you," he began, "but Violet and Daisy have had a lamentable experience. Their parents died in a boating accident several months ago and they were left alone in east Texas. I decided to assume the responsibility of guardian since I'm their closest living relative. Their father was my only brother; I have no sisters. Their mother was an only child. I've undertaken a task that's a little disquieting to me—rearing two little nine-year-old girls. They're twins."

"You are a psychiatrist, aren't you?" asked Lila,

happy for the opportunity to challenge Jason. "I would think you'd feel quite adequate for the job."

"Theory is no substitute for practice, Ms. Drake," he retorted and continued his monologue. "I'd like them to attend Smith Academy in the fall, but their test scores are too low. That's why we need your help." He put his drink down and stared out of the window.

"I know," said Lila. "A couple of hours twice a week should prepare them for their tests in the fall."

"The counselor at the academy suggested everyday," he remarked in a low controlled voice as he began pacing the floor again.

"Everyday! I don't think I can . . ." Lila couldn't find the words to complete her objection. She sighed and placed her glass and plate on the table.

"We need you everyday, Ms. Drake." The demanding tone returned to Jason's voice. He stopped his pacing and planted himself directly in front of her.

"It's such a long drive. . . ." Lila's head began to swim as she became aware of the demands Jason was making on her time. She certainly didn't want the job so badly that she was willing to jeopardize her opportunity to become a writer by using all of her time commuting to and from the Tobias home.

"Move in here. We have plenty of room," he offered and resumed pacing the floor once more.

"I couldn't possibly do that," said Lila unnerved by the thought of being so constantly close to this overbearingly assuming man. However, she realized it would be the sensible thing to do.

"Why not?" he asked. "You're with your aunt

temporarily, aren't you?" Lila could see that Jason was determined to have things his way, but she was just as determined to make arrangements to please herself. She didn't want him to feel he could maneuver her at will, and so she stood her ground.

"Yes. Her place is much too small for two people," Lila answered calmly. "I intend to find a place of my own." She had talked herself into this situation and she decided she would just as easily talk herself out of it.

"When?" his interrogation continued.

"Very soon," Lila answered triumphantly, feeling she had finally won the battle.

"Then until that time," Jason said icily, "consider this your home." He turned looking defyingly at her, his seductive lips pulled tight against his perfect white teeth.

Lila's protest was interrupted by the children entering the room.

"Hi, Uncle Jason."

"Good afternoon, girls," he answered turning to look at them. "Ms. Drake, I'd like you to meet my nieces Violet and Daisy Tobias. Girls, this is Ms. Lila Drake. She'll be living with us for the summer to give you daily lessons in math and reading. Would you like that?"

"Yes." Four large brown eyes turned on Lila and hesitantly lit up. Again Lila opened her mouth to protest but Violet interrupted her. "You're pretty," she said, "I'm glad you're going to live with us."

"Where will you sleep?" asked Daisy.

Things were moving just a little too quickly for

Lila and she realized the situation was now completely out of her hands.

"I think the rooms overlooking the garden and the pool should suit Ms. Drake," said Jason. "What do you girls think?" He smiled self-assuredly.

"You mean the one next to your room?" asked Violet.

"That's the one," he answered starting out of the library.

"Oh, that's a pretty room," the girls said. "Let's show it to her."

"All right," Jason agreed, leaving the room with the girls following close behind him. Lila remained standing in the library unable to impede the incredible developments.

Jason turned looking at her displeased. "Something wrong?" he asked arrogantly.

"Yes, terribly wrong. I don't think it would be proper for me to live here." Lila's confidence shot up. She had grasped at one last straw and she knew it was a good one.

"Ms. Drake," Jason began, but Lila interrupted him.

"Please call me Lila," she said, tired of the sarcastic way he called her by her surname.

"Lila," he repeated, "You must remember that Aunt Katherine lives in the house with us as well as Mr. and Mrs. Cobine, who are housekeeper and yardman. There will be nothing improper about your living here. Come. Please."

Lila stuffed her hands into her skirt pockets and followed them.

They led her into the entry hall and up the grand wood-carved staircase. At the top they turned left and walked down a long hall entering a door with a beautiful stained-glass panel. The room was huge and simply decorated in white and dusty rose. The king-sized bed was made with white eyelet dust ruffle and spread. Four large pillows in matching white eyelet shams were stacked at its head. Above it hung a pastel painting of sail boats. A highboy was against one wall and a matching night stand sat next to the bed. To the left and down three steps was a sitting room with a white sofa, two wicker chairs with dusty rose pillows and a white wicker desk and chair. Green plants of various sizes were arranged through-out the rooms.

"Come and see the pool," invited Violet as she stood holding the curtains away from the windows.

Lila walked across the room conscious of the thick dusty rose carpet beneath her feet and looked out onto a lovely rose garden with beautiful evergreen shrubbery and a large inviting pool.

"Do you think you can manage to live with us for three months Lila?" asked Jason, this time with a note of hopefulness in his dark eyes and deep voice.

Lila felt hopelessly trapped by the offer as she remembered her promises—to do all she could to help the twins—to the aunts. She could not possibly tell them now that she had changed her mind because she found Jason to be an arrogant cad and preferred not to ever come in contact with him again. Therefore, instead of giving him an emphatic "no," she heard herself answer "yes."

"Oh, good," the girls said embracing her. She

leaned over and gave each one a warm hug and peck on the cheek.

"Aren't you going to kiss her, too, Uncle Jason?" asked Daisy mischievously.

"That's a grand idea." Jason deliberately walked over to Lila and slid his arms around her small waist. Her breath caught in her throat as she felt his warm soft lips press against her cheek. His personal perfume mixed with expensive cologne jolted her senses giving her such pleasurable sensations that she quickly pulled away from him.

"Now you have to kiss him back," Lila heard one of the girls say.

"That idea is even better than the first," Jason said waiting, his arms still tightly wound around Lila's waist, for her to reciprocate.

She stretched up to kiss him, both hands pressing hard against his lean chest to prevent too much body contact, and Jason, recognizing the opportunity, quickly met her lips with his.

The girls giggled and pulled Lila by the hand out of the room. "When will you move in?" they wanted to know.

"I don't know," Lila said dreading the prospect of living in the same house with the arrogant Jason Tobias.

"Why don't you make it this weekend?" asked Jason. "Do you have very much to move?"

"No, just my clothes, typewriter and a few other personal things."

"Good, the girls and I will come to get you Saturday morning."

"I have a car," Lila managed to say, determined

27

not to allow this man to develop the habit of manipulating her completely.

"I'm very much aware of that," he said, "but is it large enough to move all of your belongings?"

"No," she retreated.

"Then the girls and I will come at eight to help you."

"Nine," she said, trying to maintain a little control over her life.

"Nine it shall be." His lips pulled into a broad smile.

Chapter Two

The move had gone smoothly, thought Lila as she hung her shirts, dresses, slacks and skirts in the spacious walk-in closet and arranged several shoe boxes on the top shelf. Her dozens of colored T-shirts went into the drawers of the highboy, as well as an abundance of delicate lingerie. She set up her typewriter on a portable typing table and rolled it into the small closet in the sitting room. Her novel, with its several revised chapters, was placed on the desk along with a ceramic jar full of pencils and pens. She gathered up her cosmetics and other toiletries and started toward the bathroom that she was to share with Jason.

She was disappointed she would not have this lovely red and white bath to herself, however, Jason's was in the process of being renovated and would not be completed for quite some time. She stepped into the warmly decorated room and her eyes immediately focused on the freestanding antique red bathtub which completely dominated one of its corners. The matching red washbasin was set in a large cabinet that was also a make-up table and the toilet had a room of its own. A glass shower was in a nook opposite the tub and a white chaise lounge and table were placed in front of a marble fireplace. Lots of flowers and plants were everywhere. Wall and ceiling mirrors doubled the size of the elegant chamber making it appear enormous. Lila smiled as she arranged her bottles and jars on the make-up table feeling she would spend a number of happy hours in this place. She turned to go back to her rooms and her arm brushed against the make-up table causing a perfume bottle, which was sitting precariously on its edge to tumble to the floor. The top flew off the small crystal container spilling its sweet contents. Disgustedly, Lila mopped the liquid from the floor with a tissue.

"What's going on?" Jason asked from the open door. "It smells terrific in here."

Lila turned and saw Jason casually leaning against a wall watching her. "I've been a little clumsy, I'm afraid," she said. "I've spilled my favorite bottle of perfume."

"It smells like my favorite, too," Jason replied, smiling flirtatiously. He shifted his weight from one foot to the other exhibiting a lean muscular body clad in snug-fitting white pants and an equally snug-fitting navy blue knit shirt. "It's time to knock off for lunch," he said. "What would you like to eat? I'm treating." He tried to make eye contact with Lila, but she kept her eyes averted trying to think of a logical reason to politely avoid his company.

"I hadn't given lunch much thought," she said. "I'm not very hungry now." She finished cleaning the floor and walked into the hall.

"You will be by the time we get to Sea Isle Restaurant on Galveston Island," he persisted, following her.

Although the idea of lunch on Galveston Island greatly appealed to Lila—she had always enjoyed the resort and had not been there in six years—she did not care to be in Jason's company. "It's kind of you to offer to take me to lunch," she said, "but I think I'll finish my unpacking and have lunch later."

"You're being awfully unsociable Ms. Drake," he said, blocking the path to her rooms. "I think a nice lunch together on Galveston Island should help us start the summer off just right."

"I don't think that's necessary," Lila said, trying to go around him. "I'm sure we'll manage the summer fine without having lunch together today."

"I won't take no for an answer," Jason said, moving in front of her.

Lila thought for a moment. Possibly she had been too hasty in judging Jason. He had been under a great deal of pressure recently, assuming the responsibility of rearing his nieces and finding a suitable tutor for them. Maybe that pressure had caused him to act caddishly earlier. Perhaps lunch with him today would be enjoyable and reveal a more positive side to his personality. "All right," she said, "you've talked me into it."

Jason smiled triumphantly. "Let's go." He gestured toward the stairs with his head.

Lila pulled herself up to her full height and deliberately looked into Jason's dark eyes. "I must change first, Jason," she said softly. "Give me a few minutes." She was determined not to allow him to order her about.

"Fine. I'll give you ten." He started down the hall toward the stairs.

"I'll need more time than that," Lila called after him, resolved to convey to this man she would not be treated like a child.

"But of course," he spat arrogantly over his shoulder. "See you in *twelve* minutes, Ms. Drake," he added, and his felinelike strides took him down the grand staircase and out of sight.

Lila went to her rooms wondering if she had made a dreadful mistake in accepting Jason's luncheon invitation. She was in no mood to either be bossed or have her intelligence and emotions toyed with today. She needed a refreshing and enjoyable afternoon and hoped Jason would allow her to have one.

He was certainly a capricious man, she thought

taking a change of clothes from a drawer. This morning he had been quite agreeable following her instructions for moving her belongings. However, now he was acting as if he didn't have a considerate bone in his body. Jason's irregular personality was clearly more than she cared to cope with at the present time. She would have lunch with him today, but would not involve herself with him further socially. She had to keep her mind uncluttered so that she could successfully work with the twins and finish writing her book.

Lila hurriedly changed into a pair of white short-shorts, a red tank top and slipped her feet into a pair of flat white sandals. She had wanted to tie her long auburn hair back with a ribbon but decided not to take the time, consequently, it hung loose about her shoulders. She rushed out to meet Jason.

"You're three minutes and twelve seconds late," he said sarcastically as she got into the car.

"Sorry, your majesty," Lila shot at him. Her eyes hung on his face as she recalled her Aunt Margaret telling her that Jason was thirty-five years old. She noted the heavy lashes framing his large dark eyes, a strong square jaw and his slightly full lips. She couldn't help but remember how tender and warm those lips had felt against her own. Her reverie was broken, however, when he started the car and headed toward the freeway.

"Did you bring your swimsuit?" he asked eyeing her.

"Yes," she answered, putting her tote in the back seat.

"Good," he said, "I'm sure you'll enjoy the gulf."

Lila rested her back against the door and pulled her long, smooth legs up and folded them under her. "I hope so," she said. Jason turned for a moment allowing his dark eyes to scour her naked flesh.

"Don't lean against the door," he ordered, "that's dangerous." She scooted her body forward coming closer to him. "That's even more dangerous," he said, not taking his eyes from the road. She turned in her seat, stretched her legs out in front of her and gave him a long cold look. "That's better," he said softly.

Lila was silent as her mind drifted back to the morning activities and the twins. Jason had permitted them to help her move from her Aunt Margaret's to her new quarters. Violet and Daisy were helpful bright little girls with terrific senses of humor. They had moved small articles quickly and carefully while telling "knock, knock" jokes at which they had all laughed heartily. The girls were a delight and Lila knew that her relationship with them would be rewarding.

The sun blazed down on the maroon Mercedes as it made its way toward the island. "Everything looks so different," Lila said after a long silence. She was observing new shopping centers and residential areas strung along the highway.

"Houston has grown quite a bit in the last few years," Jason answered. "The population now is well over two million people and everyday people move here to seek their fortunes. The economy is healthy and the city is also progressing in the arts. I guess there's something for everyone in Houston now."

"Yes. I can see that," Lila replied. "I think that's one reason I've decided to live here again. It's growing up to be quite a sophisticated city and yet it is managing to maintain a bit of its folksy atmosphere."

"You're right," Jason agreed. "It's a lovely place to live and I'm glad you've come back."

Lila did not respond to Jason's last statement, but silently questioned what he had meant by it. The remainder of the drive was pleasant and she welcomed the smell of the salty sea air as they drove over the causeway that connected the island with the mainland.

The historical island of Galveston was located fifty miles from Houston in the Gulf of Mexico and was one of Lila's favorite resorts. She loved the miles and miles of clean sandy beaches and the streets lined with oleanders which ranged in color from deep scarlet to pure white. The carefully restored mansions, cottages and cathedrals brought its history alive for her and she was pleased to be back on the island again.

Jason drove to Sea Isle Restaurant on the famous gaslit Strand. Once inside the small rustic building they were seated at a white clothed captain's table set for two. After much discussion of the menu they ordered lunch—deviled crabs and trimmings—and ate leisurely, savoring every mouthful. "Have you always lived in Houston?" Lila asked, curious about Jason's past.

His mood was relaxed and friendly. "No," he said. "I attended college on the West Coast and after graduation I lived there for a while before coming back to Houston to set up my practice."

"The west coast sounds like fun."

"It was but I wasn't able to establish the type of practice there that I wanted."

Lila wondered if that was the only reason for his move back to Houston. "You must find your work very satisfying."

Jason looked at Lila intently. "My work is very important to me," he said. "For the past three years I've specialized in marriage counseling and my partner and I are quite pleased with the success we've had."

The meal was delicious and Lila was happy she had accepted Jason's invitation for lunch.

Afterwards they strolled along the Strand, which was once the "Wall Street of the Southwest," peeking in shops and galleries. They thoroughly explored the area and then drove to Seawall Drive where they rented a surrey with fringe on top. They rode along the scenic ten-mile seawall for an hour, enjoying the prevailing sea breeze and the interesting sights. "Are you ready for a dip in the gulf?" Jason asked as they climbed back into the car.

"Your timing is perfect," Lila said, "I'm more than ready." They drove to one of the pocket parks along the seawall.

"We can change into our swim suits here," Jason said. They got out of the car taking their totes with them and went in the dressing rooms. Lila slipped her tanned svelte figure into her purple and green bikini and pulled her hair up in a knot emphasizing her large brown almond-shaped eyes, a small nose and thin lips. She went out to meet Jason.

"I'm over here." Jason waved to her. He had pulled on a pair of navy blue swim trunks that complemented his brawny physique. "Interesting," he said, his eyes pursuing Lila. "Don't you ever take off those gold chains and earrings?"

"Never," she replied indignantly. "They're my signature."

His eyes clung to her for a moment.

"You need no signature, Lila," he said softly. "You're unparalleled with no ornamentation." He picked up the blankets, totes and small cooler containing a couple of bottles of white wine and led the way out on the beach. Jason's words were now chisled on Lila's brain and they continued to reverberate through her mind as she walked.

"Let's go in the water," she said to him, wanting to give herself time to think and to prevent any possibility of further blandishments which she found disarming. She wanted the temperate gulf to cool their sun-warmed skin and clear their minds, which were muddled by the scenic island and their romantic lunch.

They ran into the water splashing each other playing and laughing. They caught the waves and rode them in to shore and then went further out floating on their backs and treading water. They frolicked like small children brought to the beach on the first day of summer, and after becoming tired they slowly swam back to shore. Jason spread a blanket over the hot sand and they both stretched out on it. "How about some wine?" he asked after a while.

"I'd love some," Lila replied. He took two crystal wine glasses from a small basket, poured the wine and offered her one of the goblets.

"You think of everything," she said smiling and taking the glass from him. "This is simply wonderful." Jason moved closer to her and immediately her body became tense.

"I don't bite," he said, caressing her face slowly with his free hand.

"Of course you don't," Lila said nervously, "but I prefer that you not do that."

"Would you prefer that I do this?" Jason put his glass down and took her face in both his hands. His kiss was gentle and warm and Lila found herself submitting to him. He took her glass from her, placed it next to his on the sand and began kissing her again this time pressing her slender body hard against him. A small groan escaped Lila's lips and Jason's kisses grew more ardent. His hands began to caress her neck and back while his lips clung hungrily to hers.

Suddenly, Lila felt something cold and wet against her foot and she jumped causing Jason to release her. A chubby little puppy was investigating their belongings and had pulled some of their things out of their totes. Jason turned to chase the dog away and knocked over the wine goblets making them fall against each other and break into small pieces. "I'd better get this up," he said picking the glass from the sand.

Lila was grateful to the little puppy for his mischievousness and shuddered at the thought of how easily she had surrendered to Jason's lovemaking. "I'm going to take a walk, Jason," she said, welcoming the opportunity to get away from him for a while.

He looked at her curiously. "Wait until I finish this," he said, "and I'll go with you."

"No, I'd much rather go by myself," she said determined to give herself time to think away from him.

"Please yourself," he said tightly and turned away.

She walked slowly away down the beach. The breeze off the water seemed to settle her nerves and cool her inflamed emotions. Her heartbeat was back to normal and she fought all thoughts of the recent incident from her mind. She walked aimlessly picking up sea shells, odd pebbles and driftwood. Occasionally she glanced out to sea at the ocean liners in the distance. She knew she could not allow Jason to kiss her again. That would be destructive.

"Would you like something to put those in?" a stranger with sparkling blue eyes held out a bag toward her. He was deeply tanned, lean and muscular and his youthful face indicated he was in his early twenties.

"Yes, thank you." Lila accepted the bag and placed her small treasure in it.

"I'm Ron, the beach patrolman," he said pushing a lock of blond hair from his face.

"Oh, hello, I'm Lila."

"I see you like shells and driftwood. Do you use them for making things?" he asked.

"No, if they're pretty or interesting I just pick them up and display them where I can enjoy them."

"I see. I collect shells and driftwood too, but I make things from them. I've sold some pieces, but basically it's a hobby."

The beach was peaceful and Lila and Ron walked along the edge of the surf searching for objects of interest and chatting.

"Are you all right?" Lila heard Jason ask over her shoulder.

"Yes. I'm fine," she answered, surprised he had followed her. "This is the beach patrolman, Ron," she said. "Ron, this is Jason Tobias." Courtesies were exchanged.

"Ron and I are looking for shells and driftwood."

"Oh, really?" asked Jason eyeing the other man.

Silence settled over the threesome. Lila did not want to be alone with Jason just yet and so she stood glued to the sand trying desperately to think of something more to say. Suddenly Jason snatched the large beach towel from around his neck and wrapped it around Lila tucking it in tightly at the waist covering her from her waist down to her ankles. Stunned speechless she looked up at Ron. His complexion had turned a deep crimson, his eyes widening to twice their size. Humiliated, she stormed away, clenching the bag so tightly in her fingers they began to ache. Instantly Jason was by her side; she yanked the towel from her body and flung it in his face.

"What was that all about?" she demanded angrily.

"Dear Ron was having eye problems."

"So what if he was?" she asked fuming and walking faster.

Jason kept up with her with easy strides. "It's my responsibility to protect you from leering men."

"And just when and why did you assume such a responsibility?"

Jason grabbed her by the shoulders and pulled her to him forcing her to look up into his face. "The moment you got into my car and I brought you here I assumed responsibility for you," he said. "And I'm especially responsible for you when you come in contact with lascivious old men."

She pulled away from him. "Poor Ron is neither lascivious nor old," said Lila, a little amused at Jason's choice of words.

Silently they walked back to where they had left their things. Jason grabbed the blanket, folded it quickly and gathered up his tote and cooler.

"Are we leaving now?" Lila asked watching him. His mood had changed and he acted as if she was not standing beside him.

"Yes," he answered coolly, "I have to get back to Houston." They changed and headed toward the car. The little puppy that had disturbed them earlier came from nowhere and ran behind them barking. They tried to chase him back to the beach thinking someone would be looking for him but he would not go. He sat wagging his tail and looking at them with his tongue hanging out. They began to walk away and again the puppy followed them.

"I'll take him to the beach patrolman," Lila said,

handing her belongings to Jason and taking the puppy in her arms, "it's dangerous for him to be in the parking lot." She had a soft spot in her heart for the little animal that had saved her from succumbing to Jason's desire.

"I'll go with you," he said putting the things in the trunk of the car. They went to the patrolman's office and knocked on the door. Ron opened it and looked at Jason skeptically.

"This little puppy seems to be lost," Lila said, handing him to Ron. "I'm sure someone will be looking for him soon."

"On the contrary," Ron said taking the dog, "Cherries is the one that's doing the looking."

"What do you mean?" Lila asked puzzled.

"Cherries is just a mutt that someone abandoned several months ago," Ron said stroking the pup. "An old gentleman down the road took him in and has been caring for him since that time. But now he's too expensive for the old man to feed, so he asked me to help him find a home for him."

"Oh, Jason," Lila said, "would Violet and Daisy like a puppy like Cherries?"

"Maybe," Jason said reaching for the pup.

"He should be no trouble," Ron said, "he's had all of his shots and as you can see he's a friendly little fellow."

"Why do you call him Cherries," Jason asked.

"I don't know," Ron responded, "the old man named him."

Jason thought for a while and then spoke, "We'd like to take him for my nieces. I'll pay you for him."

"The old man wouldn't dream of taking money for the dog," Ron said. "All he asks is that you give him a good home."

"We will," Jason said, "and thank you. By the way," he added after hesitating for a moment, "I'm sorry if I caused you any embarrassment earlier."

Ron shrugged his shoulders and smiled. "No, problem," he said.

Jason put the puppy in the back seat and opened the door for Lila. She paused for an instant. "It was good of you to apologize to Ron."

"You noticed?"

"I noticed," she said. "You've given me the courage to apologize to you, Jason. I'm sorry for losing my temper."

"Really?" he asked amused. "I accept your apology. And maybe since we're doing all of this apologizing I should also apologize to you, although I can't imagine why."

"You can't even think of one reason?"

"Not one," he quipped encouraging her into the car and slamming the door, a trace of a smile playing on his lips. He walked around the front of the car to the driver's side, slid under the wheel and turned the ignition.

"You're a cad, Jason," Lila said angrily.

"I know," he answered, smiling fully, but no other words were exchanged during their drive back to Houston.

Jason pulled into the drive next to a red convertible. He took their things from the trunk of his car and went in the house. Lila followed him, carrying

Cherries in her arms and wondering who owned the fancy sports car. They went to the kitchen and found the twins and Mrs. Cobine there, engaged in a game of Monopoly.

"A puppy," the girls said excitedly when they saw her. "He's so cute." They took him from her arms and began petting him. "We didn't know you had a puppy, Lila."

"I don't," she answered happily. "He doesn't belong to me. Your uncle brought him for you. He's yours."

"Thank you, Uncle Jason," they said, too busy playing with the little dog to look at him.

"You must thank Lila, also," Jason answered. "It was her idea to bring him to you girls."

"Thank you, Lila. Does he have a name?"

"His name is Cherries," Jason answered, "but I suppose you can change it if you like."

"That's a cute name," the girls said. "Don't you think so, Mrs. Cobine?"

"It's a lovely name, girls," the housekeeper answered. "Here, let's give him some milk." She filled a bowl and placed it on the floor. They watched fascinated as Cherries lapped the milk from the dish.

"Oh, there you are, darling," an attractive brunette said, walking toward Jason with her arms outstretched. "I thought I heard you drive up. Did you forget that you invited me to dinner tonight?"

Jason embraced the woman and kissed her lightly on the lips. "Of course not," he said. "Nikki, I'd like you to meet our house guest and tutor for the twins, Lila Drake. Lila this is Nikki Jocksay, my colleague."

44

"Oh, this is the new help," Nikki said, eyeing Lila and hanging onto Jason's arm. "How nice."

Mrs. Cobine cleared her throat noisely. "How many for dinner, Mr. Tobias?" she asked. "And what time would you like it served?"

"Have the girls eaten?" Jason asked.

"Thirty minutes ago," she answered.

"Then it will be three for dinner, Mrs. Cobine," he said, "and we'll eat in twenty minutes."

"I hope you're not including me, Jason," Lila said, not wanting to tangle with the haughty Nikki Jocksay, "I can—"

"Of course I'm including you," he snapped and left the room with Nikki trailing close behind him.

"Don't let her scare you none," Mrs. Cobine said, "freshen up Ms. Drake and enjoy your dinner."

Back in her rooms Lila was sure the day would never end. Having dinner with Jason and his girl friend was the last thing in the world she wanted to do tonight. It was puzzling that he had introduced her as his colleague when it was obvious they were more than work associates. And to think he had kissed her on the beach today. The man was impossible. Well, she was hungry and she did have to eat. *She wouldn't allow Jason to ruin her day and her health,* she thought angrily. She would join them for dinner.

She brushed her hair and pulled it tight behind her head in a chignon and slipped a pale yellow and white silk stripe dress over her head that complemented her sun-kissed complexion beautifully. She stepped into her white high-heeled sandals and went down to dinner.

Jason and Nikki were already at the table when Lila entered the dinning room. He eyed her appreciatively as she took her seat. Mrs. Cobine served the salad. "I hear you're writing a book," Nikki said, looking across the table at Lila. "What is it about?"

"It's a romantic novel," Lila said dryly, not wanting to be interviewed by Nikki.

"Fiction?" she asked, as if the work suggested something dirty. "How disappointing," she looked at Lila through heavily mascaraed lashes, "I thought you were writing something that required talent. Something factual."

"Dear Nikki," Jason said amused, "how can you dismiss Shakespeare, Sartre, Mitchell and other distinguished writers of the genre so lightly?" He looked at her intently waiting for an answer.

"Oh, darling, I wasn't putting them down," she said, embarrassed after realizing what she had said. "I just thought maybe Lila was doing something that required research and study." She laughed nervously. "I'm sure she's a very talented girl," she added.

"Of course," Jason said.

Mrs. Cobine took their salad plates and brought in the baked chicken and carrots. They completed their meal with fresh fruit and a more agreeable topic of conversation. After dinner drinks were served in the library.

"Dinner was perfect," Nikki said to Jason as she sat on the sofa and crossed her legs seductively. "It was nice and light—just what I need for my figure." She flashed him a syrupy smile.

"Yes, we can see you have a weight problem."

Lila's words were dipped in the same jar of honey as Nikki's smile and she felt thoroughly vindicated for the snide remarks the woman had made earlier about her writing when she noticed the red color crawl into the brunette's face.

"Please excuse me," she said, rising from her chair. "I must go work on my book."

Chapter Three

Lila relaxed in the antique bathtub with her eyes closed and her head resting against its high back. She had filled it to the brim with hot water accented with lemon fragrant bath crystals. She took several deep breaths, let them out slowly and felt her muscles relax. After making a rich lather with an oval bar of lemony soap and a soft cloth, she gently massaged her body. With deliberation, she rinsed the soap from her skin, then relaxed against the back of the tub again. Her mind gradually reviewed the week and the routine the household had established.

Her day usually began with a swim in the pool, after which she had breakfast with Ms. Katherine and the twins. She would then tutor the girls and two hours later leave them in the care of Mrs. Cobine. Daisy and Violet were good students and Lila enjoyed teaching them.

After tutoring sessions, her time was her own and she spent most of it at the typewriter. Her writing had gone well during the week and now she looked forward to taking a break. Having dinner with her Aunt Margaret and Hunter was just what she needed and she anticipated a pleasant evening.

Reluctantly Lila stepped out of the tub and dried herself briskly with a huge bath towel.

Aunt Margaret and Ms. Katherine were leaving the following Friday on a European tour for several weeks and this would be the last evening she would have with her aunt until her return. She knew she would miss them both, but was happy they lived such active and full lives.

She slipped into her bathrobe and went to her rooms to dress.

The only time Lila had seen Jason during the week was when he joined the family for dinner on Wednesday night. Their encounter had been friendly and they had lingered over coffee discussing the program that she had developed for the girls. Lila had been relieved when she realized chance meetings in the house with Jason were slim, for he was extremely busy and out most of the time. His absence made things easy for her because she did not have to spend valuable time thinking up schemes of how to best avoid or outmaneuver him. She assumed he loved and spent his time with Nikki Jocksay and smiled when she thought of how much they seemed to deserve each other.

Lila pulled a lilac and apricot silk print dress over her head and the soft fabric clung provocatively to her full bosom and trim hips. She put on a pair of high-heeled taupe leather sandals and applied a small amount of shadow to her eyes and gloss to her lips. Her hair swung loose and full about her face in soft bouncy curls. She took one last look at herself in the mirror, tucked a small natural straw bag under her arm and left the room.

Because Lila's car was in the shop for repairs, Aunt Margaret had agreed to pick her up for the evening.

"How lovely you look, my dear," Ms. Katherine said when Lila entered the library.

"You're simply beautiful," her Aunt Margaret commented. "Shall we go?"

"I'm ready," Lila replied.

"How will you get back, Lila?" asked Ms. Katherine.

"Don't worry," the young woman answered, "Hunter will drive me home."

"Of course," Ms. Katherine said, "then have a good evening," she added and saw them to the door.

Hunter arrived for dinner with wine and red roses. Aunt Margaret was delighted to see him and their reunion was happy and warm. They talked about old times for a while and then had the savory dinner that the women had prepared. Lila noted Hunter's happy mood and it warmed her heart. She hoped their friendship would grow and was happy that now she had a friend in the city—especially since Aunt Margaret was going away on a holiday. They had just completed their meal and were having wine in the living room when the doorbell rang.

"Would you get that please, dear?" Aunt Margaret asked Lila.

"Certainly," Lila said going to the door and opening it. Startled, she stood staring at Jason. "Why are you here?" A cynical smile pulled at his lips.

"Aren't you going to invite me in?" he asked.

"Yes." She stepped aside, "come in, Jason," she said unwillingly. He followed her to the living room where he greeted Aunt Margaret and was introduced to Hunter.

"Have some wine with us, Jason," Aunt Margaret invited.

"I'd love to." He sat in the chair opposite Hunter's. Lila gave him a glass of wine along with a cold disapproving look.

"I didn't know your dinner guest was your boyfriend, Lila," he said, returning her insulting glance. Hunter's face colored as Jason continued, "But Aunt Katherine was concerned about your getting home and asked me to pick you up. Had I known you were dining with Hunter I never would have bothered."

"Nonsense," Aunt Margaret said hastily, "we're

pleased you've joined us. And do let's set the record straight," she added, "Hunter is an old family friend—not Lila's beau."

"Indeed," Jason said surveying the younger man.

Lila resented her aunt explaining her relationship with Hunter to Jason, but understood she had done so because Hunter was a married man. Nevertheless, the whole situation had made her angry so she left them to entertain each other while she tidied up the kitchen. It was perplexing that Ms. Katherine had asked Jason to pick her up when she had clearly explained to her that Hunter would drive her home. She thought again of how anxious Aunt Margaret had been to "set the record straight" as she had called it, and wondered if the two ladies were trying to play matchmaker. She shuddered at the thought. "I think we should let you get some rest now," she said to her aunt when she rejoined them.

Hunter rose from his seat, went over to Aunt Margaret and kissed her lightly. "It's been a lovely evening," he said. "Thank you for inviting me. And don't forget," a thin white finger was pointed at her, "I'm looking forward to hearing all about your trip when you get back."

"Good," Aunt Margaret replied happily, "that'll give us a valid reason to have another party." They all laughed, said goodbye and the three young people left together.

"I'll see you two next week at the party," Hunter said as they walked to their cars.

"What party?" Lila asked surprised.

"Jason's party Saturday night," Hunter said, baffled by her reaction. "He invited me while you were in the kitchen. You will be there won't you?" he asked.

"Absolutely," Jason answered for her, "she lives there."

"Terrific. I'll see you then." Hunter got into his car and drove away.

Jason had driven a short distance down Westheimer Road before Lila spoke. "Thank you for the gracious invitation to your party, Jason," she said caustically. "I'd love to attend."

"You're welcome," he replied, and they eyed each other icily.

Jason drove a little farther and then turned into the parking lot of a small night club. "Why are we stopping here?" Lila asked.

"You need to relax before going home," he said, "I'd hate for Aunt Katherine to know that her concern for your welfare made you angry."

They sat in a small booth in a corner and Jason ordered white wine for both of them. "You know that isn't true, Jason," she said. "I appreciate Ms. Katherine's concern, but I don't understand why she asked you to pick me up when I told her right before I left that Hunter would be bringing me home."

The drinks came and they both began to sip them slowly. "I thought you knew our aunts have plans for us." He smiled at her sardonically. "But I can see you didn't," he observed. "However, if I had known you were having dinner with an old flame tonight, I never would have intruded. When Aunt Katherine asked me to pick you up, I automatically assumed you were dining with one of your aunt's lady friends." His dark eyes searched her face. "Silly of me, wasn't it?"

Lila was taken aback by Jason's words. "Hunter is not an old flame and you can tell the aunts to forget it."

"But of course. We both know that the very idea of the two of us together is absurd." Jason's eyes grew narrow as he leaned across the table. "You're enticingly beautiful tonight, Lila," he said. "Were you successful in your attempt to bewitch poor Hunter?"

She stared at him blankly.

"I said were you . . ."

"I heard your question, Jason," she snapped, "and I don't like the implications."

"It doesn't matter whether you like the implications or not. Just answer the question."

"Hunter is a married man, Jason," she hissed through tight lips. "I'm only interested in his friendship."

"So why did you wear that dress?" he threw back at her. "And why didn't you invite his wife to your little dinner party?"

"I happen to like this dress," she said, "that's why I bought it. And I didn't invite his wife to dinner because they're separated." She felt disgusted with herself for revealing Hunter's personal life to him.

"I see," he said thoughtfully and relaxed in his seat.

"Would you please take me home, now," Lila said to him.

"Certainly." For a long time they rode in silence.

"Why did you invite Hunter to your party?" she asked.

"Because I knew it would be a sure way of getting you there."

"It's unfair to use people that way, Jason," she said. "And besides, why would you want me there? Did Nikki refuse your invitation?"

"Nikki will be there," he said matter-of-factly, "and so will you."

She bristled at his self-assured attitude. "I told you my living in your home wouldn't work, Jason," she said, "and you've just proved me right. I can't accept your ordering me about or your intrusions in my personal life. Additionally, I will not tolerate you abusing my friends. I'm moving out as soon as I can find a place."

"Are you through?" he asked.

"Yes," she answered tartly.

"I think you've forgotten your primary reason for moving into my home," he said, "but if you choose to leave and abandon your responsibilities to Violet and Daisy, which is what I predicted you would do, then I will gladly help you pack and move."

His words struck like sharp knives as she realized again Jason had outmaneuvered her. "I won't leave Violet and Daisy," she told him, "nor will I truckle to your every whim."

She detected Jason's suppressed smile and silently regretted ever meeting him. "Are we still pretending to write?" he asked, swinging the car into the drive.

"I'm doing very well with my writing," she said coolly, "thank you for your interest." She got out of the car and rushed to the door intending to let herself in with her key, but realized because she had not driven her MG she had neglected to put her keys in her purse.

"Waiting for something?" Jason asked when he joined her at the door.

"I forgot my keys."

Amused, he walked over to the swing on the porch and sat down. "I'm not going in just yet," he said.

She followed him to protest and he pulled her down beside him. "Is this necessary, Jason?" she asked wearily.

"Yes, *this* is very necessary," he said and drew her to him. The heat from his body assaulted her and the sweetness of his kiss caused her arms to involuntarily encircle his neck. Her mind told her to pull away from him, but Lila found herself pressing her body against his long muscular frame and hungrily returning his kisses. His hands roamed slowly and skillfully over her face, neck and shoulders and she could feel his heart thumping against her breast. *The fire that he was causing to race through her veins would surely consume her,* she thought and she pulled away from him and went to the door. "Please, Jason," she said, "I want to go inside."

Slowly he walked over to her, opened the door and they went in together. At the foot of the stairs he took her in his arms and kissed her gently. "Good night, Lila," he said. She clung to him for a moment and then ran up the steps aware of his dark eyes following her.

Lila's second week in the Tobias home was significantly different from the first. Although Jason made no further advances toward her, he had begun having both breakfast and dinner with the family—which pleased Ms. Katherine tremendously. At first his presence had disturbed Lila, but she quickly regained control of her senses and her days became productive and happy once more.

On Friday afternoon the two aunts left for Europe and they had all gone to see them off. The girls became caught up in the excitement of the airport and wanted to know if they could take a vacation also. Jason promised if Lila felt they were doing well enough in their studies to take a break by the middle of the next month he would consider it. They were thrilled and promised to work twice as hard in the coming weeks.

The music was light and breezy and the crowd noisy when Lila made her entrance at the party. It was in full swing as she searched the crowd for a familiar face and spotted Hunter. She pushed her way through the throng of people to him.

"I was beginning to think you weren't coming," he said, slipping his arm around her waist.

"I almost didn't," she confessed. "Jason knows a lot of people, doesn't he?" she asked, glancing around the room.

"Yes, it's a nice group." Hunter looked at her admiringly. "You look lovely, Lila."

"Thank you." She slipped her hands into the pockets of her mint green and white chiffon strapless evening gown.

"Would you like to dance?" he asked.

"Why not?" Hunter guided her around the floor

to a slow but rhythmic love song. Her eyes caught Jason's for an instant, but she pretended not to see him as she relaxed in her friend's arms. Occasionally she smiled up at him and he returned her smiles warmly.

"I haven't danced in years," he said after the music had stopped.

"You're still good at it," she complimented him.

"Well, well, well," Jason said, coming over to them, "welcome to the party, late bird." He handed her a glass of champagne and his lips curled sarcastically. "I was beginning to think you had decided to be antisocial tonight."

"Looks like a nice party, Jason," Lila said perfunctorily, giving him a side-long glance. "And I do think things were so arranged that my presence would be guaranteed." Her smile was candied.

"Hello, Lila," Nikki said joining them and slipping her arm through Jason's. "It's so sweet of you to come to my birthday party."

"Your what?" Lila was shocked and looked from Nikki to Jason disbelievingly.

"Yes, didn't I tell you it was a party to celebrate Nikki's birthday?" Jason asked casually. He furrowed his brow. "It must have slipped my mind."

"Jason is such a dear," Nikki cooed. She turned to Lila wide-eyed and asked, "Aren't you going to wish me a happy birthday?"

"Happy birthday," Lila said coolly.

"I think it's time everyone wished you a happy birthday." Jason silenced the crowd. "It's time to sing Happy Birthday to Nikki," he announced and began singing. Everyone else joined in. Mrs. Cobine brought in a large cake and the brunette blew out the candles and cut it into small pieces. Jason started the music again and took Nikki in his arms. The floor was cleared and they danced a samba, smiling and looking deeply into each others eyes. Everybody was laughing and applauding when Lila slipped through the crowd and made her way to the kitchen.

"Enjoying the party, Ms. Drake?" Mrs. Cobine asked.

"No," Lila said flatly. "If I had known this was a party for Nikki I never would have come." She sat at the counter with the housekeeper.

"Oh, that's no reason not to enjoy yourself," the older woman said, "ignore Ms. Jocksay and dance with some of the nice young men that Mr. Tobias has invited."

"All the young men that Mr. Tobias invited were lining up to dance with the birthday girl when I left," Lila said, "I think I'll go to my room and work on my book." She slid from the stool and walked toward the door.

"I'm sorry to see you so unhappy, Ms. Drake," Mrs. Cobine said, "and I want you to promise me you'll stop working so hard and playing so little." She smiled broadly, but Lila could see concern written on the woman's face.

"I promise, Mrs. Cobine, but it would be more work than play if I attended this party. Good night." Lila walked up the stairs and to her room without being seen.

She tried to concentrate on her work, but the only thoughts that came to mind were of Jason and Nikki holding each other and dancing. She walked over to the windows and looked out at the warm clear night. Lila thought she had never seen so many stars in all her life. A light tapping at the door startled her.

"I had to show the housekeeper my I.D. before she'd tell me where you were," Hunter said smiling. "She thought you might like this." He produced an ice bucket with a bottle of champagne in it from behind his back and two glasses.

"Oh, great," Lila said happily. Her spirits lifted. "Come over and sit down." They went to the sitting room and opened the champagne. "I'm sorry I left the party without telling you," she apologized, "but you were having such a good time I decided not to bother you."

"Yes, I'm having a terrific time," Hunter said. "I haven't been to a party like this one in years. I'm glad Jason invited me. He seems to be a great guy."

"He does, doesn't he?" Lila commented, thinking if Hunter really knew what she thought of Jason he would be very surprised.

"Are you tired?" He smiled and handed her a glass of champagne.

"A little."

"How's the book coming?"

"I'm doing very well with it," Lila felt relaxed and happy talking about something that was so dear to her heart. "If I stick to my schedule, I'll complete it by mid-August."

"That's wonderful. You'll have to give me an autographed copy when it's published." Hunter took a sip of his drink.

"I will," she promised. They talked for several hours before a knock at the door interrupted them.

Lila opened it and Jason entered the room. His body tensed and his dark eyes grew narrow with rage when he saw Hunter.

"So you're having a private party," he said closing the door behind him.

Lila was surprised to see him and even more surprised at his attitude. "What I do in my room is none of your concern, Jason," she said.

"Quite the contrary," Jason countered, "everything that goes on in this house is my concern. I don't appreciate you entertaining men in your bedroom, Ms. Drake. It's a bad example for my nieces."

"I hardly think that what you see here could rightly be called entertaining *men* in my room," Lila said growing angry.

"We were just having champagne and talking," Hunter said. He was stunned that Jason had become so enraged over such an innocent situation and tried to placate him. "It was a wonderful party, Jason," he added. "Thanks for inviting me." He glanced at his watch and realized he and Lila had been talking for hours. "Are all of the other guests gone?" he asked.

"Yes. The party is over, Mr. Matthews," Jason said turning on Hunter savagely. "Whatever you've been doing in here will have to end." He glared at the younger man contemptuously.

"How dare you come in my room and make ugly accusations," Lila said.

"What other conclusions could one draw coming in and finding you two this way."

"What way?" she demanded.

"I missed you and Hunter hours ago and thought

he had gone home and you had come to your room," he said. "What have you been doing in here all of this time?"

"Oh, how little your mind is, Jason," Lila said, "how very, very small." She walked to the door and flung it open, "Get out!"

Mrs. Cobine, who had been to check on the twins before going to bed, was coming down the hall. "Are you all right, Ms. Drake?" she asked coming over to Lila. She could see anguish in the young woman's face and turned to the men when she spoke again. "Perhaps you should leave," Mrs. Cobine said. She helped Lila slip out of her evening gown and crawl into bed. "Try to sleep now," Mrs. Cobine coaxed her, "things won't seem so bad in the morning." The housekeeper left her and Lila tried to fall asleep but found it impossible. The recent events kept flashing across her mind like bad scenes on a motion picture screen. She got out of bed and began pacing the floor when a soft knock, which led her to believe Mrs. Cobine had come back to see if she was all right, caused her to rush to the door and open it. Her eyes met Jason's.

"May I come in?" he asked.

"I'm not allowed to entertain men in my room," Lila said blocking the door. The nightgown she wore did little to conceal her body and Jason's eyes wandered over her freely, stopping here and there taking in delectable points of interest.

"Stop it," she said taking her bathrobe from the foot of her bed and pulling it on. "What do you want, Jason?"

"I want to talk to you."

"We have nothing to discuss. I think you expressed your feelings perfectly the last time you were here."

"I was irrational."

"Yes you were, and it wasn't the first time. But I suggest if you want me to remain here, you make it your last."

"You're not considering deserting the ship again," Jason asked concerned.

"No, Jason," she said, "I'm not leaving the girls. I will complete the job I've started with them, but you will have to accept the fact that you are the girls' guardian and not mine. Stay out of my private life." She watched Jason's face—which told her nothing—and waited for his retaliation, but his response was much different from what she had expected.

"I'm sorry for my behavior tonight, Lila," he said evenly. "I had no right to speak to you the way I did. Forgive me." He moved toward her but she walked to the open door.

"What about Hunter?" she wanted to know. "You must have made him feel awful."

"I'll call him tomorrow and apologize," he promised.

They stood looking at each other for a moment. Both seemed too tired to fight any further. Jason started out of the room, "I think I'll go for a swim," he said. "Join me?"

Lila looked at the bedside clock. "It's four o'clock in the morning!"

"I know," he replied, "but the exercise will relax you so you'll be able to get some sleep."

"I can sleep fine without swimming with you," she said tartly.

"You're still upset." His voice was soft but persistent. "A swim will do you good."

Lila moved closer to Jason and spoke to him directly. "You have twice been successful in pointing out to me that I owe it to Violet and Daisy to remain here as their tutor as I promised at the beginning of the summer. I have assured you that I intend to keep that promise. It is not necessary that you invite me to any of your social functions and especially early morning swims to get me to remain in this house and do my job. All I ask is that you treat me with respect."

"I respect you," Jason said, assuming the same cool attitude as her own, "and don't think for one minute I'm trying to bribe you into staying here by inviting you to anything. However, I do think for the sake of the aunts and the twins we should try to be friends. A swim now will do us both a lot of good."

Lila considered refusing his invitation but realized she needed to make some effort to help reconcile their differences. Furthermore, the idea of relaxing the tight muscles in her abdomen and getting some sleep appealed to her, so she decided to accept his offer. "I'll meet you at the pool," she said.

She slipped into a white bikini and went quietly down the stairs and out of the house. A soft warm breeze caressed her body as she lowered herself into the water. The stars and moon were the only light there was and the only light that was needed. She began swimming the pool's length and wondered why she had never tried late night swimming before.

The experience was exhilarating. She heard the water slice and within seconds Jason was beside her. They smiled at each other and continued to swim. After a while Lila pulled herself up on the side of the pool to rest and the warm breeze cooled her wet skin. Jason swam over to her. "Tired?" he asked, playing with her toes that dangled in the water.

"Yes," she confessed laughing.

"I'll rest with you," he said and climbed up beside her. The moonlight played upon their wet hair and skin, making them glow as if they were creatures from another world.

"Do you swim late at night like this often?" Lila asked. "I love it."

"All the time. I do some of my best thinking swimming at night or early in the morning."

"It is morning, isn't it?" Lila said.

"It's morning and you're beautiful." Jason took her in his arms and their skin touched, setting sparks flying like fireworks on the 4th of July. His lips found hers and they willingly parted. Her small hands roamed over his broad muscular shoulders and arms inflaming her as well as Jason and their wandering did not cease until her fingers dug deep into his wet curly hair. He picked her up without breaking their embrace and carried her to one of the lounge chairs beside the pool. He put her down gently, stretched out beside her and pulled his lips from hers allowing his eyes to caress her face, neck, shoulders and breasts. His eyes were like torches and Lila cried out softly as she reached out for him to put out the fire that he had ignited in her. Jason pulled her to him and she melted away in a swoon. His lips covered her face with kisses and they stopped momentarily to drink deeply from the sweet well of her warm parted lips. He continued his glorious attack as his burning lips found her neck and shoulders and branded every inch of them marking his ownership. She tried to pull him closer and he skillfully flipped her over and began a slow exquisite assault down her spinal column. Craving to press her small body against his hard lean frame once more, she turned in his arms and their lips fused like heated metal. Lila opened her eyes to search Jason's face and the bright morning sun temporarily blinded her. "It's morning," she said, tearing herself away from him and standing shakily by the lounge chair.

"We discovered that sometime ago," Jason said holding on to her hand and pulling himself up.

"I know, but it was still dark then," she told him. He held her against him tenderly. "The sunrise is beautiful."

"Just like you," he answered, taking her face in his hands and kissing her lightly on the lips. They walked to the house and up to their rooms hand in hand. "I'm glad you came swimming with me, Lila," he said, and pressed his lips against her forehead. He left her at her door and went to his rooms.

Although Lila had found the early morning swim refreshing, she knew it had been a mistake to allow Jason to be so intimate with her. He was still very much involved with Nikki Jocksay and their relationship seemed to be a serious one. She crawled into bed and when she closed her eyes this time the picture that came into focus was of Jason holding her in his arms. She dozed off and when she awoke again the sun was high. Lila glanced at the clock. It was noon. She jumped out of bed, showered quickly and dressed in an aqua and navy blue cotton skirt and an aqua T-shirt. She put on a pair of navy blue flat sandals and pulled her hair up in a ponytail. A small noise from her stomach reminded her she had not eaten since the day before at dinner. She tidied her room and went down to find something to eat.

Chapter Four

"Well, you're certainly bright and chipper this morning," Mrs. Cobine observed when Lila walked into the kitchen. "I told you things would look better after a good night's sleep."

"I feel fine," Lila answered happily, "however, I am a little hungry."

"Everything will be ready in just a few minutes," the housekeeper said. "The twins are changing and as soon as they're dressed I'll serve dinner. The

Sunday paper is in the library if you'd like to glance at it while you wait." Lila went into the library expecting to find Jason there, but the room was empty. She picked up the paper and turned the pages absently. Shortly, her daydreaming was interrupted with the twins' announcement: "Mrs. Cobine says you can come to dinner now."

"Wonderful," Lila said, stopping to take each girl's face in her hands and kissing her. "I'm starved." They went into the dining room and took their seats. "Isn't Jason joining us?" she asked, looking at the three place settings on the table.

"Uncle Jason isn't here," Violet answered. "We met him going out when we were coming in from church."

"You've been out?" Lila asked.

"Yes, we've had breakfast, been to church and read the comics," Daisy announced. "And Lila, you're just getting up. You're a sleepy head." They laughed.

Mrs. Cobine brought in the mixed-greens-and-watercress salad. "You shouldn't have gone to all of this trouble, Mrs. Cobine," Lila said, "the three of us could have eaten in the kitchen."

The housekeeper looked shocked.

"Oh, no, Ms. Drake," the housekeeper said emphatically, "Mr. Tobias has always insisted that meals be served in the dining room, even if he or his aunt are not present."

"Of course," Lila replied. "When will Jason be back?"

"I'm not sure," Mrs. Cobine answered, "he did

mention to the twins, however, that he probably wouldn't get back until after they had gone to bed tonight."

"I see." Lila felt a sharp pain pierce the pit of her stomach. "Then I guess we're left to entertain ourselves today," she said to the girls.

"Did you forget, Lila?" Daisy asked. "We're going to Mary Ann's birthday party this evening. Mr. and Mrs. Cobine are taking us." They looked at her questioningly.

"Yes, I did forget," Lila said thoughtfully. "Looks like I'll have to entertain myself." Her smile was broad but weak.

The girls' big expressive eyes were concerned. "We can stay home with you Lila, if you like," Violet said.

"You will do no such thing," she replied, moved by their compassion. "I have a thousand things that I need to get done today. Don't worry, I'll be okay," she assured them. Mrs. Cobine brought in the roast ducklings with stuffing and green peas and they completed their meal with cheesecake and happy chatter.

The day was too beautiful for Lila to remain inside so she climbed into her MG and began driving aimlessly. She found herself on US 290 and drove through the small towns of Prairie View and Navasota. The scenery was lovely, which helped to take her mind off Jason, and by late afternoon she turned onto a road that led her to Washington-on-the-Brazos, the state park which is considered the birthplace of the Texas Republic. Lila got out of the car and toured the Star of the Republic of Texas Museum. From the museum she walked next door to Barrington, a ·house furnished with early Texas period pieces and then took the footpath to Independence Hall and watched a slide presentation on Texas history. She talked a little with some of the other people touring the park and then drove back to Houston, arriving just after dark. The house was quiet when she let herself in and Lila, tired from her long drive, showered and went to bed.

Days passed and again Lila had to adjust to Jason's wayward attitude. His presence in the house had once more become irregular and when she did see him, it was usually at mealtime with his attention focused on the girls. She wondered how he could forget their magic rendezvous at the pool just a couple of weeks ago, and realized she had been a fool to think he had taken her seriously. When Hunter called and invited her out for dinner and a movie on Thursday night, she had gladly accepted.

Dinner at Don's Seafood Restaurant was ideal and the movie, a comedy, had been just what Lila needed. When Hunter brought her home, instead of going inside they had sat in the porch swing talking. Before long the maroon Mercedes pulled into the drive and Jason got out. He greeted them cordially, exchanged a few pleasantries and went in the house. Shortly thereafter, Hunter left and Lila went inside.

Jason was in the living room—heard her come in—and asked her to join him. She accepted his invitation along with a tall cold glass of lemonade that he offered her.

"Did you enjoy your evening?" he asked, relaxing on the sofa and sipping his lemonade.

Lila braced herself for the argument that she knew was sure to follow. "The evening was superb," she exaggerated.

"Good," Jason said dispassionately. "When I spoke with the twins this morning they asked to go to the theater in the park to see *Peter Pan* tomorrow evening. I promised I would take them and wondered if you'd like to join us?"

Surprised and somewhat hurt that he had not challenged her about going out with Hunter she answered truthfully, "That sounds wonderful, Jason. I'd love it." Their eyes locked for a moment and she wondered if he had some ulterior motive for inviting her, but quickly decided if he did she could adequately handle it. "I'll prepare a picnic basket and we can have dinner in the park before the play begins."

"I was hoping you would suggest that," he said, "otherwise it would be a mad rush having dinner someplace else and getting to the theater on time."

"Would you like anything special?" she asked.

"Whatever you prepare," Jason said, "will be perfect." He walked her to the foot of the stairs, pecked her on the cheek and went across the hall to the library. Lila went to her rooms and spent the majority of the night working on her book. Jason's perplexing attitude toward her caused her to make more typographical errors than usual.

The next evening Mrs. Cobine helped her pack the picnic basket with French bread, sliced baked chicken, potato salad, makings for a green salad and dressing, fruit and cheese. "This should go with the meal just perfectly," the housekeeper said, and placed a bottle of white wine in the cooler.

"You're a romantic, Mrs. Cobine," Lila replied. The older woman smiled and put a few cans of fruit juice on ice for the twins.

The park was crowded when they arrived and finding a suitable location for their meal was difficult. However, they managed to set up their picnic atop a hill that gave them an excellent view of the theater stage. After dinner the girls, catching sight of Mary Ann and some other friends, ran off to play. Lila and Jason lolled on the grass and watched the crew set up the stage.

"I've been thinking of taking the twins on holiday for two weeks," Jason said casually. "What do you think?" he turned to look at her.

The first thing that came to Lila's mind was the thought that the girls had to be ready for their exams by the end of August and their readiness was her responsibility. That fact dictated her answer. "Two weeks is a long time, Jason," she said, "that's at least twenty hours of lessons. Why not take them away for two or three days."

"That won't give me sufficient time to do what I'd like to do," he said frowning.

Jason's capriciousness was not only limited to her,

Lila thought, *but he was also changing his mind concerning the welfare of his nieces.* When she first met him his primary interest was their education. Now it seemed he had switched his concentration to their recreation. "What is it that you'd like to do?" she asked.

"I'd like to explore the Mexican Caribbean Coast with them," he said, "and I'd especially like them to see some of the Mayan ruins."

"That would be terrific."

"Yes, I think they'd enjoy it, and the experience would be an education in itself. However, the trip would require more than two or three days and I must confess, I'd like a little time just to relax in the sun."

"I hate being the one to discourage such a wonderful vacation," Lila replied mindfully, "but twenty hours is more time than we can afford to lose."

Jason stretched completely out on his back with his hands cushioning his head. "I'll hate to tell the girls that you're the reason they can't have a vacation," he sighed, looking longingly into the distance.

"That's not fair, Jason," she said trying to make eye contact with him, but he continued to stare at the setting sun. She took his face in her hands to force him to look at her and turning his head, he kissed her palms. Lila jerked her hands away from his mouth as if she had been burned and fought the fire that his lips had sent coursing through her body.

"There is one way you can prevent being blamed for the twins missing a beautiful two week vacation in the sun," he said, aware of the emotions he had aroused in her.

Knowingly, she took the bait. "How?" she asked.

"Go with us?" He turned over and pulled her into his arms.

"That would be impossible," she said emphatically and wiggled out of his grip.

The twins ran over to them excitedly. "The play is about to start," they said, "where are the tickets?"

"Calm down." Jason dug in his pockets "I have them here." They found their seats just as the first characters came on stage and like most plays at Miller Theater, *Peter Pan* was excellent.

When they got home Mr. and Mrs. Cobine were in the back yard and Daisy and Violet went out and enthusiastically told them all about *Peter Pan*. Mrs. Cobine gave them cookies and milk then got them ready for bed. Lila went in the kitchen to put away the leftover food from the picnic and Jason followed her.

"What have you decided about the vacation?" he asked, walking up behind her and wrapping his arms around her waist.

"Jason, please," she said, "someone may come in and get the wrong idea."

"I've put everyone to bed," he laughed, and his warm moist lips found the nape of her neck.

"When do you plan to go?" she asked, attempting to distract him from her vulnerability.

"Maybe the end of next week." He allowed her to turn in his arms so he could look in her face. "Do you think you can be ready by then?" He held her close.

"I'm not going with you, Jason," she answered, "but what I will attempt to do is give the girls four hours of lessons a day until we make up the twenty hour loss."

"No." Jason released her and took a pitcher of iced tea from the refrigerator. He filled two glasses and handed her one. "Cramming is no good. Their lessons should be properly spaced."

"That's the best I can do," she said drinking the iced tea.

"It's not good enough," his voice was low and angry.

"I realize you're used to having your way, Jason," Lila said, "but I'm afraid this time it's impossible. Accompanying you and your nieces on vacation wasn't part of our original agreement, and I don't see the necessity of working it into my plans at the moment."

"We'll discuss it later," Jason said coolly, "there's something more important that I must speak to you about." He sat at the kitchen counter and Lila took the stool next to him. "I don't want you to see Hunter anymore this summer," he said plainly.

His words hung in the air like a dark threatening cloud and Lila's eyes slowly found his face and fastened on it in wonderment. "You're doing it again, Jason," she said, not wanting to believe the nerve of the man. "Are you now attempting to pick and choose my friends for me?"

"No, I wouldn't be that presumptuous," he said arrogantly. "I'm making a simple request—don't see Hunter again for a while."

With the same cool haughtiness Lila replied, "I will see whomever I like whenever I please." She slipped from the stool and started out of the kitchen, but before she could reach the door Jason caught her by the arm and pulled her to him. "I'm quite serious about what I'm asking you to do," he said through clenched teeth. With his large strong hands he pressed her small body against him.

"And I'm quite serious when I tell you I'll do as I please," she retaliated, trying to extricate herself from his grip, but her movements against his hot muscular body only served to set them both on fire. Their lips met in a flaming penetrating kiss and their hands caressed each other frantically. Lila could feel herself losing control and with great determination wrenched away from Jason. Her shaky legs somehow carried her up the steps and into her rooms.

A cool shower helped her calm her emotions and after dressing for bed she went to the windows to look out at the clear warm night. A splash in the pool diverted her attention and she watched Jason gracefully glide through the water. Later he stretched out on the deck to rest and the moonlight and shadows played chase upon his skin. Reluctantly, Lila tore her eyes from him and climbed into bed.

The sound of footsteps rushing back and forth outside Lila's rooms woke her up. She slipped into her bathrobe and stepped out into the hall. Jason was hurrying stone-faced toward the twins' room and Lila ran behind him. "What is it?" she asked him. "Has something happened to Violet and Daisy?"

"They have upset stomachs," Jason said, not

turning around, "and very high temperatures." Lila followed him to the girls' room and found Mrs. Cobine there with them.

"Why didn't you call me?" Lila asked, hurt that they had not let her know the girls were sick.

"We didn't think it was necessary," the older woman said, holding Daisy in her arms, "but I'm glad you're here now." Lila went over to Violet's bed and began mopping the child's body with a cloth. The two women stayed with the girls the remainder of the night and by morning they were better and sleeping peacefully.

A week passed before the twins were up and about. They had missed ten hours of lessons and Lila was pushed to find some way to make up the lost time. The girls were still weak from the virus and unable to cope with their regular work schedule. Lila had wanted to discuss the problem with Jason, but wasn't in the mood for an argument so she decided to call Hunter for an evening out instead.

For the first time since they had renewed their friendship, Hunter declined to spend an evening with Lila. His explanation—a demanding work schedule—was puzzling because in the past he had used the very same reasoning for taking a break. Lila doubted that Jason's threat and Hunter's polite refusal were coincidental. However, she decided she would say nothing to either man about it. If Hunter ever wanted to see her again, he would have to call her.

Reluctantly, she resolved to go in and talk to Jason about the twins. He looked up from his desk irritatedly when she walked into the library. "I'm sorry to disturb you," she said, "but we need to discuss the children's work." Jason leaned back in his chair and looked at her for a moment then walked from around his desk and sat on the sofa. He looked tired. His eyes had circles around them as if he had not slept in days, and his movements were slow and laborious. "You've been working too hard, Jason," she heard herself say softly.

He looked at her in surprise. "I didn't know you cared." He raised his hands above his head, stretching his tall frame.

"About Violet and Daisy . . ." she quickly said.

"Yes, let's *do* discuss Violet and Daisy," his smile was warm and teasing.

"We've lost a lot of time. I'm afraid your vacation plans will have to be cancelled. Also, I'll have to work with the girls for at least three hours a day for a while." She waited for the explosion.

"I don't think the children should be punished for getting sick," he said calmly.

"Of course not," Lila replied, "but we can't forget our primary objective for them this summer either."

Their eyes met and held for a second. "Why can't we combine vacation and work, Lila?" he asked.

She got up from her chair and began pacing the floor trying hard to think of a good explanation. Lila knew she was objecting to going with them on vacation not only because of her determination not to allow Jason to manipulate her at will, but also because she was afraid of her feelings for him. She could not allow him to abuse her affections. However, she realized it would be unfair to deny the children such an ideal trip because of her own insecurities. "All right, Jason," she said, "we'll try it your way."

He took her face in his hands and kissed her tenderly on the lips. "Thank you. The trip will be good for all of us. I'll make arrangements and give you the details in a couple of days. You won't be sorry," he added, smiling. She left the library feeling that she probably would.

Chapter Five

This alone was well worth the trip, thought Lila happily as she looked out at the clear blue waters of the Pacific Ocean and the fine white beach that bordered it. She placed a chair in front of a window —which expanded the width of the room in the El Presidente Hotel—and relaxed concentrating on the view. It was exquisite. Sail boats could be seen in the distance, as well as the heads of snorkelers moving lazily through the water. The beach and the sea were inviting, but Lila chose to remain in her room.

She had never been to Mexico before and was glad she had decided to come to the resort city of Cancun with Jason and the girls. Her excitement had not ignited until she had boarded the plane and thumbed through a book on the area. She could understand now why Jason had chosen to vacation there and was looking forward to taking some of the many interesting tours that were available.

Jason had thoughtfully reserved a single room for her so that she could comfortably continue to write on her book, a room for the twins and a room for himself. There was no reason for the two weeks ahead not to be enjoyable.

Lila took a cold drink from the refrigerator in her room and resumed her position in front of the window. She had helped the girls unpack and put on their swimsuits and they had gone with Jason to the beach. From where she sat she could see them laughing and playing together in the water. As she sipped her drink she thought of how thrilled Mr. and Mrs. Cobine had been when they learned she was going with Jason and the girls on holiday. She suspected they too were in favor of the matchmaking efforts of the two aunts. Right now, however, her feelings concerning Jason were ambivalent. She could not deny she was very much attracted to him, but Lila resented his demanding wayward attitude. Also, she realized, his relationship with Nikki Jocksay was still in question and knew she had to keep her emotions in check or she could be hurt very badly.

By the time Lila had completed her unpacking and her cool drink, Jason and the girls were back from the beach. They made plans to rest for a couple of hours before dinner. Everyone set their travel clocks and Lila crawled into bed and had no problem falling asleep.

After dinner in the hotel dinning room, Jason and Lila took the girls for a stroll around the grounds. They found a lovely little area close to the pools and sat at a table and planned their activities for the next day. Daisy and Violet—too excited to sleep earlier—were tired and Lila went up to their room with them to help them prepare for bed, agreeing to meet Jason in the hotel bar as soon as she had finished. The girls slipped into their pajamas and got in bed and before Lila could turn the light off they were asleep. The day had been long and exhilarating.

Lila went to the bar and found Jason sitting on the balcony with a chilled glass of white wine waiting for her. "I think the occasion calls for a toast," he said smiling warmly. Lila picked up her glass, turned to him and waited. "To the most perfect holiday ever." Their eyes held for a moment and then they slowly drank from their glasses. "Well, what do you think?" Jason asked gesturing and looking around him.

"I think this is one of the loveliest places I've ever visited."

"Are you glad you came?" he asked.

"Yes," she answered simply. They talked for a long while about organizing their activities during the trip before Jason moved closer to her and began playing with her gold hoop earrings. His large warm hands caressed her face gently in the process and he allowed his fingers to wonder down her throat and become entwined in her gold chains. He leisurely massaged her neck and back.

Lila drew back from him and quickly picked up her drink to protect herself from his amorous advances. "It's getting late," she stammered, "and we have a long day planned for tomorrow." Without another word Jason walked her to her room, kissed her tenderly on the lips and sauntered away.

When the alarm clock sounded Lila rolled over and turned it off. A couple of seconds elapsed before she remembered she was in Cancun and not in her dusty rose and white rooms in the Tobias home in Houston. Her eyes fluttered open and took in the heavy Mexican furniture with the natural fabric's yellow and orange accents. She got out of bed and opened the drapes, revealing a beautiful sunny morning. Lila lingered at the window a while before taking a cool shower, which served to complete the job of waking her up. She put on a lilac scoop-necked T-shirt, a deep purple skirt and a pair of medium-heeled backless sandals. She left her hair loose and curly about her shoulders and went next door to tutor the twins.

Violet and Daisy had dressed themselves in khaki shorts and white T-shirts and were waiting for Lila when she knocked on the door. She tutored the girls for an hour and scheduled their second hour of work during siesta. They went directly across the hall to Jason's room and found a note on the door instructing them to meet him in the lobby. He was sitting in a huge over-stuffed chair reading a magazine when they reached the spacious open air foyer crowded with new arrivals. "Ready for breakfast?" He rose from his seat as they approached.

"Yes, we're hungry," the twins answered.

"Good, breakfast here is supposed to be a gourmet's delight." They went into the large multileveled dining room which was decorated with fishnets, shells and large colorful paper flowers. The enormous glass windows admitted the brilliant Mexican sun which washed the room with its golden rays. The blue-green sea could be seen beyond the hotel grounds and swimmers were already gliding out toward the horizon.

American and Mexican breakfast dishes were laid out on buffets and Jason, Lila and the girls joined the line to serve themselves. Lila and Jason chose mostly native dishes and encouraged the girls to do the same. They were then escorted to a table that overlooked the sea. Breakfast was indeed a delight.

After breakfast, Jason kept his promise and rented motor bikes to ride into Cancun City. Violet rode with Lila, who had biked through many European countries, and Daisy rode with Jason. They followed Cancun Boulevard out of the resort area across the bridge and into the city which was approximately ten years old. Cancun was interesting because it had been scientifically planned by the Mexican government with the use of computers and was probably the first city designed and built using that method. The city's primary purpose was to provide services for the resort area which was laid out beyond the bridge along the lagoons facing the ocean. It was constructed around several public parks and Jason led the way to one so they could have a rest.

Later, they leisurely made their way through the narrow side streets of the city exploring small gift shops and buying inexpensive clay and papier-maché souvenirs. They found their way back to Cancun Boulevard, and cruised across the bridge passing several of the luxury hotels situated there. Jason, who was leading the way, turned his bike on to Chac Mool Beach. Lila followed him. "Let's get a cool drink," he said, walking over to the open air restaurant. They ordered their drinks and took in their surroundings, the bluest water in the world and its clean, white-sand trimming. It was a magnificent sight. Jason explained that the beach was called Chack Mool Beach after the Toltec Indians' god of sacrifice. He pointed out a statue of the god that sat on the beach with the offertory in his stomach.

The girls walked over to get a closer look at the statue; Lila and Jason remained in the restaurant. "I'm glad you persuaded me to come with you," Lilà told Jason, allowing her eyes to follow the girls. "I'm having a terrific time." Lila felt as long as they stayed involved in specific activities there was no danger in her becoming too involved with Jason.

"I am, too." He reached for her hand and enfolded it in his. "I've made arrangements with the hotel babysitting service to have someone keep an eye on the girls tonight while we see what the town has to offer after dark." Lila felt herself flush. She had just clarified how to best deal with Jason on this holiday and now he was tempting her to complicate the situation. She wanted to go with him and yet she realized the invitation held serious danger for her.

Jason sensed the conflict she was having with her emotions. "You'll enjoy it," he said smoothly.

"I'm sure," she smiled. "Isn't it about time for siesta? Let's get back to the hotel." They made their way back to the hotel and went in for their nap, after which Lila tutored the girls for an hour. She slipped a note under Jason's door telling him she and the girls had gone down to the hotel swimming pool. They played in the pool until late evening and then dressed for dinner.

Lila slipped into a light blue sun dress which revealed all of her back and plunged seductively in the front. She put on her white high-heeled sandals and left her hair loose to dry naturally. Their lobster dinners were superb, and Lila and Jason left the twins in their room with instructions to be in bed by ten o'clock. They got a taxi and went to La Burbuja, a night club in Hotel Camino Real, one of the luxury hotels on Cancun Boulevard.

The club was packed with tourists and native residents who thoroughly enjoyed the floor show—a young, handsome Mexican who sang mostly popular American songs. After the show a band played lively music and Lila and Jason danced until early morning. They decided to walk back to the hotel, which was at least a couple of miles away. The night was warm and breezy and they walked hand in hand along Cancun Boulevard. "That was fun," Lila said looking up at him.

"I knew you would enjoy La Burbuja," Jason answered, draping his arm around her shoulders. They arrived at the hotel and Jason walked Lila to her door, kissed her mouth tenderly and went to his room, leaving her bemused by his gentleness.

The next two days were pretty much like the previous ones, with them spending most of their time lolling on the beach. Lila, however, had been disciplined enough to work on her book and was pleased with the progress she made. By mid-week they followed their usual morning routine and after breakfast boarded the tour bus to Tulum, a Mayan Indian city of about a thousand years old.

Tulum—one of over 50,000 archaeological sites in Mexico—sat spectacularly on a cliff overlooking the Pacific. The Mayan fortress was small, containing approximately sixty well-preserved structures and dated from about 1200 A.D. Its most outstanding characteristic, a protective wall on the three land sides of the city, was unique among Mayan ruins. The fourth or seaward side of Tulum, which means wall, was protected by a high cliff. Lila was excited about seeing this place because of its unusual setting.

The tour bus pulled up to the site and everyone got off. Jason, Lila and the girls followed the English-speaking guide who led them through an entrance in the wall and to the first point of interest. They adjusted their large straw hats on their heads to protect them from the oppressive sun, and slipped into long-sleeve shirts to keep their skin from burning.

The guide gathered the people around him as he told them of a cross-shaped grave containing skeletal remains that had been discovered in the center of the structure. Beside the remains were containers holding the bones of a variety of fish, birds and reptiles. It was believed these gifts would nourish the spirit on its trip to the next world. The archaeologists called this building a funerary platform. Lila shivered visibly as she listened to the guide and momentarily she felt Jason's arm slip around her waist.

The group walked over to a structure, thought to be a palace, with a small shrine inside and a few wall paintings that could still be traced by the remaining paint. The building, which was complete until the central roof gave way in 1929, had not been officially named.

From there they went to the temple of the Frescos. It was thought to be the best preserved and most interesting structure at Tulum. The temple had had many additions; however, the initial construction was a small, low, single-roomed temple with a door facing the street. Its ceiling was curved and an altar was on the back wall. Rich wall murals, which were protected by the additions to the building, were still visible.

Moving northward, the group came to a large complex which was the second largest building in Tulum. This structure was called the Great Palace and its front section, made up of one large and one small room with a pillar in the center, was obviously newer than the back. On the left side was the main entrance where steps led up to an opening with four pillars. Beyond this entrance was a long great hall with a horizontal roof held up by a row of eight pillars running down its center. There were a couple of narrow rooms in back of the great hall with small windows in the outer wall.

The last structure that the guide escorted them to was the castle which sat almost in the center of the seaward side of Tulum. Its size dictated its name and it stood above all the other buildings in the city. Two rooms sat atop the large pyramid. The smaller room had ceremonial benches around all its sides but one and the larger room rested on two columns which displayed the heads of the god Kukulkan.

After the formal tour, they were given some time to explore the ruins at leisure and they climbed the steps that led to the top of the castle and looked out over the city. They then investigated the house of the cenote, a natural cistern used by the Indians as a source of water, the snail platform and the cliffside oratories. They made their way back to their starting point where they bought cold drinks and climbed aboard the bus. The children had enjoyed the tour and had been able to follow the lecture the guide had given. They sipped their soft drinks and discussed additional uses the Indians might have used the structures for.

Jason and Lila had enjoyed the tour also and, like the twins, they discussed the different buildings they had seen.

The tour bus turned onto a well paved road and traveled six miles south to the National Park lagoons —four crystal clear interconnecting lagoons called Xel Ha, meaning where waters are born. The park was self-contained with a gift shop, snack bar and restroom facilities. Jason, Lila and the girls changed into swimsuits and walked through the well designed park to the breathtakingly beautiful lagoons where multicolored fish of all sizes darted to-and-fro. They donned snorkeling gear, slipped into the cool clear waters and swam several yards from shore. Their view from that vantage point was spectacular—they could see the lagoon floor several feet below and the abundance of sea life that lived there. They explored the area for about an hour and found it difficult to tear themselves away from the lovely site, but the tour bus was leaving for Cancun and they had to be on it.

Their first week in Cancun was nearing an end and Lila smiled to herself as she thought of how smoothly the days had passed. *It would have been a shame,* she thought, *to have missed such a wonderful holiday because of her silly fears.* She knew she had handled Jason and her emotions quite well, and wished she could accurately assess his behavior and feelings. He seemed to have enjoyed her company this week as much as she had enjoyed his; however, she was aware of the fact that five days on a romantic tropical island was no basis on which she could judge anything. The only sensible thing for her to do would be to wait and see if his interest in her would last.

A knock at her door brought Lila's attention back to reality. Instead of typing, she had been daydreaming. She opened the door and Jason stepped into her room.

"Working hard?" he asked, coming in and taking a seat.

Happy to see him, she sat in the chair opposite his, "Not really."

"Where would you like to go tonight?" He picked

up a few of her typewritten pages and thumbed through them casually. "We can find someone to keep an eye on the girls."

"I think it would be fun to take the girls out tonight," she answered.

"Good. Any suggestions?"

"I'm sure they'd enjoy the ballet folklorico performance in the auditorium of the Parian Convention and Shopping Center. I'm told it's a colorful show, and we can pick up tickets at the door."

"Sold," Jason said, rearranging his muscular frame in his chair. "What time does it start?"

Lila found the brochure that contained the information and scanned it before she answered. "Nine-thirty."

"All right," he said, "we can go right after dinner." He studied her for a couple of minutes before he spoke again. "You seem to be surviving very well without Hunter."

At first Lila thought she had misunderstood him, but slowly his words registered and anger began to crawl through her system. "I'm not sure I understand you," she said in a controlled voice.

"You seem happy, although Hunter isn't here hanging on to your every word." Their eyes met and held. "Miss him?"

"You seem to be obsessed with Hunter, Jason," she said evenly.

"On the contrary," he quipped, a smile playing about his lips, "just making sure you're not."

"I'm not," she said sharply, uncertain as to why he had made a point of riling her. "You paint an awfully unattractive picture of Hunter," she added, "and I don't like it. He's a wonderful friend and I won't tolerate your suggesting he has such a low opinion of himself."

"I'll soon find out for myself." He rose from his seat and walked toward the door. As an afterthought he asked, "Are you in love with him?"

"Of course not," Lila answered calmly, "but tell me, Jason, why are you so determined to mar our holiday?"

"I'm only trying to get the facts straight," he said coolly. "See you at dinner." He closed the door of her room quietly behind him.

Dismayed, Lila dropped onto her bed. The five days they had shared had been lovely and now this tension had come between them. Jason surely had a reason for questioning her about Hunter, but no matter how hard she tried she could not fathom his motives. The argument had been silly and unnecessary, but still it had dampened her spirits. She would have to try to forget it. The holiday was for the girls and she had to do all she could not to spoil it for them. Mechanically she got up from the bed, showered and dressed for dinner.

The twins were excited about going out for the evening and they chatted happily throughout dinner. Conversely, Jason and Lila were quiet—occasionally their eyes met, but other than that no communication occurred between them.

They arrived at the Convention Center in time to secure four tickets for the night's performance and with many other tourists found their seats and watched beautiful graceful dancers in colorful costumes perform various Mexican dances. They thoroughly enjoyed the show and after it was over hailed a cab and went back to the hotel. Jason kissed the girls good night and reminded them they had a trip scheduled to Isla Mujeres the next morning and suggested they not delay in getting to sleep. Lila helped them into bed and then went to her own room. She knew sleep would not come easily, so she worked on her book for several hours before crawling into bed.

They boarded the Fiesta Maya, a glass bottom boat, to sail to Isla Mujeres right after breakfast. Clad in swimsuits and cover-ups they found their way to the sundeck and chose seats along the railing. The ship left the lagoon pier sailing out into the beautiful blue-green sea and at a certain point it stopped so that coral reefs and an assortment of fish could be observed through the four glass viewing stations in the lower hull. Then it started up again and finally reached its destination of Isla Mujeres— Island of Women. They disembarked the Fiesta Maya and found a cool spot on the beach, where Jason gave them a little of the island's history.

The five and one-half miles long and one mile wide island of Isla Mujeres was first seen by European explorers in 1517. The explorers' ships had been caught in a terrible storm, which caused them to drift for twenty-one days. When land was finally sighted, it turned out to be an island with statues of Mayan Godesses along the coasts—thus the explorers named the island Isla Mujeres. The next day they landed on the island after having a conference with Mayan chiefs, who later had them attacked. Some explorers were hurt, but most of them escaped. They were able to capture two Indians who later played a part in the conquest of Mexico. At one time the island was used as a hide away for pirates because of its isolated position. But in more recent times, a naval base was built there and during World War II allies used the island as a lookout post. Its beauty and isolation are now enjoyed by both Mexican and foreign tourists.

After their brief history lesson, they snorkeled in the crystal clear water but before long it was time to leave. Again the ship sailed out to sea and the band on the lower deck began to play. Lila left Jason and the girls on the top deck and went below to listen to the music. Dancers crowded onto the small dance floor and swayed rhythmically to the music as a breeze off the water circulated and cooled their heated bodies.

"Looks like fun." Jason was at her side.

"Yes, it does," she said, looking about. "Where are the twins?"

"There," Jason said, pointing to the girls who had managed to find a spot to watch the dancers. The music stopped, everyone applauded and the band began to play once more, this time a cha-cha. Jason held out his hand to Lila in the customary way a man invites a woman to dance. Surprised at his invitation, she accepted by allowing him to take her into his arms. The music was pulsating but mellow and Jason, an excellent dancer, guided Lila smoothly around the floor. Their sinuous bodies responded to the music as if they had rehearsed, and within minutes all the other couples on the floor stopped dancing and gathered around them. The long yellow, green and white matching skirt that Lila wore over her swimsuit blew in the wind, exposing her slim tanned legs and bare feet. She twirled away from Jason arching her back allowing her hair to bounce seductively about her shimmying shoulders. Their lips were pulled into broad smiles and their eyes locked as their undulating bodies continued to express the music until it ended. The people applauded. Then Jason and Lila, with the twins looking on and joined by other couples, danced until the boat docked in Cancun.

Chapter Six

Lila had spent the morning going in and out of the many elegant shops and boutiques in the Mauna Lia Shopping Center and now she sat in one of its sidewalk cafes sipping a soft drink. Her heart skipped a beat as her eyes surveyed the area and glimpsed a brunette entering one of the shops. The woman looked like Nikki Jocksay, but Lila was sure she was mistaken and allowed her heart to resume it's normal rhythm as she took another mouthful of the cool refreshing liquid. Enjoying her day alone—Jason had taken the twins to Contoy Island Wildlife Preserve by boat—she shopped and relaxed at leisure. She finished her drink and returned to her shopping, looking for a dress to wear out to dinner with Jason. They would be dining alone for the first time since their trip to Isla Mujeres and Lila wanted to look especially nice. She went to a shop that displayed a variety of dresses and chose several to try on. She finally decided to buy a long rose and white one with a soft full skirt and tiny straps. After browsing in a couple of the other shops, Lila walked to the far side of the shopping center to get a bus back to the hotel. As she walked she realized that earlier her eyes had not deceived her, for coming toward her with a broad smile on her face was Nikki Jocksay.

"Lila," Nikki cooed, slowing her pace. Lila wanted to continue walking but knew she would only look foolish if she didn't stop and speak to the brunette. "I've been trying to contact Jason all morning," she said looking about, "where is he?"

"Jason and the girls took a tour this morning," Lila responded, dismayed Nikki had intruded on their holiday.

"You *are* staying at the El Presidente Hotel, aren't you?" Nikki confirmed.

"Yes." Lila knew not only did Nikki know what hotel they were in but also their room numbers and any other information she required.

"I had difficulty understanding the gentleman at the desk when I called," she continued, "I don't speak Spanish very well but I thought I understood him to say Jason was registered there. Perhaps I'll call back and leave a message for Jason to contact me at my hotel."

"Are you on holiday?" Lila asked dryly, not wanting to show interest in Nikki but curious as to just why she was in Cancun.

"Yes, for a couple of days," Nikki answered, "and I must see Jason as soon as possible. In case he doesn't get my message," she said sweetly, "please tell him to contact me at the Camino Real Hotel."

"Of course," Lila said and walked away to get her bus.

Lila didn't want to distract Jason's attention from her or initiate an argument with him and so as she dressed for dinner she pondered how to tell him Nikki was in Cancun and trying to contact him. She had deliberately neglected to mention it earlier when he first got back from the tour; however, Lila realized it would be only right to inform Jason of Nikki's presence at the resort, in case he had not received her message. She reluctantly promised herself she would let him know sometime during the evening as she answered his knock at the door.

"The Contoy tour was fun," Jason said as they sat in the elegant Colorines restaurant in Hotel Aristos. "I missed you very much."

Warmed by his words, Lila avoided his eyes as she remembered Nikki Jocksay and her message. "I'm glad it was a good tour," she replied.

"How was your shopping?"

"Terrrific. I found an awful lot of things that I couldn't resist." She tried to tell him about Nikki but the words would not come.

They lingered over dinner for quite some time before fatigue forced them grudgingly back to their hotel. At her door Jason slipped his arms around Lila's slender body and held her close for a long while before kissing her tenderly on the mouth. "See you in the morning," he murmured against her ear and turned to go to his room.

Unwillingly Lila spoke. "Can you come in for a moment, Jason? I have something to tell you." Perplexed by the seriousness in her voice Jason followed Lila into the room and leaned against the wall waiting for her to speak. Lila walked away from him as she spoke not wanting to see the pleasure her message would bring him. "It was selfish of me not to mention it earlier," she said, "but I saw Nikki Jocksay today and she asked me to tell you to call her at her hotel—the Camino Real." She turned to receive his reaction.

"Is that it?" Jason asked looking at her blankly.

"Yes." She returned the empty look not knowing what to expect next.

A smile slowly creased Jason's face as he walked over to her and enfolded her in his arms. "My dear, dear Lila," he said, his large warm hands caressing her back, "I can't believe you've suffered all evening just because you failed to give me a message from Nikki." He cupped her chin in his hand and lifted her face to his, "It was totally unnecessary."

"Did you know she was here?" Lila asked pulling away from him. "She left a message for you at the desk."

"No," he answered. "I haven't checked the desk

for messages and the point is," he looked directly at her, "it doesn't matter that Nikki has decided to come to Cancun."

"I see," Lila said. "She did say it was very important that you contact her."

"I'll call her in the morning," Jason said, kissing her warm, moist mouth. "Sleep well, Lila," he added and left the room.

The next morning, after their usual routine, Jason allowed the twins to spend the day with friends from Houston they had met on the Contoy tour while he and Lila lounged on the beach.

"Nikki is going to join us here on the beach this morning," Jason said casually, "she needs to talk to me about a couple of things we're working on."

"Really?" Lila asked. "They couldn't wait three more days until you get back to Houston?"

"She says not," Jason answered, stretching his long muscular frame, "however, we will soon find out." Lila followed Jason's gaze and saw Nikki, in a brief red bikini, walking toward them.

"Good morning," she said happily, pulling a huge beach towel from her bag and spreading it out next to Jason, "this is a lovely spot." She turned to look at him. "Thanks for inviting me over."

"You said you had something urgent to talk to me about," Jason said. "What is it?"

"Oh, it can wait," the brunette answered, rubbing sun tanning lotion into her skin. "Let's just enjoy the morning." She positioned herself seductively on her towel and sighed deeply. "How is the little book coming, Lila," she asked, "I understand you were going to work on it while you were here."

"The little book is coming along just fine," Lila said coolly.

"Poor Jason has been without adult companionship for almost two weeks," Nikki said, stroking Jason's shoulder, "and it's about time for that to change. Why don't we go dancing tonight?" she asked him.

Lila felt a tightening begin in the pit of her stomach as she waited for Jason's answer. "On the contrary," he said, slowly adjusting his sunglasses, "Lila and I have had a great time since we've been here. It's kind of you to offer to entertain me tonight, however, I have already promised the evening to the twins."

"That's too bad," Nikki said with a note of disappointment in her voice. She turned to Lila, "What are you doing tonight?"

"Working on the little book," Lila said and rolled onto her stomach to allow the sun to reach her back.

Silence permeated their small area of the beach and gradually morning turned into noon. "Why don't you see me back to my hotel, Jason?" Nikki asked. "We can have lunch and talk there."

They gathered their belongings and headed toward the hotel. "All right," Jason agreed, "wait for me here in the lobby while I change. I'll only be a minute." He and Lila took the elevator up to their rooms. "You don't mind being left alone for lunch do you?" he asked.

"Of course not," Lila replied smiling, "I just hope

Nikki doesn't work you too hard. This is your vacation from work."

Jason returned her smile and kissed her lightly on the lips. "Don't worry," he said, "it's probably not much of anything that she wants to talk to me about." He left her at her door and went to his room.

The next morning they boarded the bus to take their last tour of the holiday and what was promised to be the most exciting. Chichen Itza, the largest and most well preserved archaeological site in the Yucatan, was the aggregate of the Mayan and the Toltec-Itza civilizations. The area was too vast to explore in one day; however, they were scheduled to see some of its most fascinating highlights. Chichen Itza dated from about 1,000 B.C. to 1461 when it was abandoned by the Toltec-Itza Indians. Its architecture was phenomenal and the first building that their guide took them to was El Castillo or the castle. The structure, the largest at Chichen Itza, was a seventy-eight-foot-high four-sided pyramid. Each side of the pyramid had a flight of ninety-one steps and a small platform rested on its top. The combined steps and platform represented the 365 days of the year. It was assumed that the building was dedicated to the worship of the god Kukulcan.

The guide gave them the opportunity to investigate the structure and Lila, Jason and the girls along with other tourists climbed the ninety-one steps to the top of the pyramid. The view from that vantage point was thrilling and they took the time to snap each other's pictures against the spectacular background. They explored the top of the building thoroughly and then began their decent—which was more of a challenge than the climb. The steps were so steep and narrow that to look straight down at them they seemed almost nonexistent.

From there they went to the sacred cenote or well. Many articles and artifacts had been brought up from the well, supporting the theory that it was used to sacrifice people to the gods. Lila felt Jason's arm steal around her shoulders and found it comforting.

They were shown several other interesting buildings and the last one they saw was the ballcourt. This structure was designed to accommodate a game, which was also a religious rite. The object was to get a ball through either of two stone rings set twenty-three feet from the ground. Evidence indicated the winner—the one who got the ball through the ring—got all the clothing, jewelry and ornamentation of the spectators and the losers were decapitated.

They were given time to further tour the area on their own, but before long they had to board the bus. The long, hot trip had been interesting and when the bus made its way back to the hotel it was time for siesta.

"This has been a well planned and diversified holiday, Jason," Lila said as they walked to their rooms. "I've enjoyed it very much."

"I knew you'd like the area," Jason said, "and it has proved to be just what I wanted for the girls. We successfully combined work and play—thanks to you, Lila."

"I never dreamed it would turn out this well," she replied.

"I was positive if you gave it a chance it would work."

"I'm glad I did." They reached the twins' door and saw them in. "Take a shower and go straight to bed," Lila instructed. "We'll skip our afternoon lesson today and I'll knock on your door for dinner."

"All right," the girls obeyed.

"Where will we have dinner tonight?" Lila asked as Jason walked her to her room. This would be their last night in Cancun and she looked forward to sharing it with him.

Jason stopped short. "I must have forgotten to tell you," he said. "I'm having dinner with Nikki tonight."

"Our last night together in Cancun?" Lila asked with disappointment written on her face.

"I'm sorry, Lila," Jason began, "I didn't realize . . ." Lila's angry words stopped him.

"It's quite all right, Jason," she snapped. "The girls and I will have a lovely meal right here in the hotel. Enjoy your evening with Nikki." He tried to embrace her but she pulled away and went in her room.

At dinner Lila was relieved the twins were tired. She did not have to press herself to be entertaining. Although deeply hurt by Jason's choice of companions for the evening, she was determined not to let his whimsical behavior get her down. She helped the girls pack before going to bed, since their flight back to Houston was leaving the following afternoon.

They told her how happy they were she had come with them on holiday and how very much they had enjoyed the trip. At that moment, she remembered she had agreed to come to Cancun to give the girls the opportunity to have a vacation as well as continue their lessons. Her purpose had been fulfilled and she knew she should be satisfied with that knowledge. But her interest in Jason and his relationship with Nikki kept her from enjoying the moment. Again she wondered why Nikki had come to Cancun and why Jason had not mentioned their discussion, although he had had plenty of opportunities. She forced herself to push them to the back of her mind and went to her room to pack.

Lila had been sleeping fitfully for an hour or so when a soft tapping at her door roused her. "Who is it?" she asked through the locked door.

"It's me," Jason answered softly, "let me in. I have to talk to you."

"I'm in bed, Jason," she said, "we can talk in the morning."

"I want to talk to you now."

"No."

"Either open the door, Lila," he threatened, "or I'll break it down."

Slowly she turned the lock and opened the door and Jason pushed into the room past her. When she switched on the desk lamp her eyes fastened on to his firmly set jaw, clenched fists and searching dark eyes. He moved toward her and she took a step backward. Losing her balance she fell on the bed. Before she could get to her feet again Jason was beside her pinning her shoulders down with his large strong hands. "Let me up, Jason," she said feeling herself becoming impassioned by his nearness.

"Not until you explain this sudden change of attitude," he said.

"*My* change of attitude?" she asked bewildered. "I didn't leave you and the girls to have dinner with someone else."

"Nikki and I are business partners. You know that."

"Could the business have waited until your return to Houston tomorrow?"

"Yes," he said hesitantly, "but since she was here I decided to clear up a few things that called for my attention. It slipped my mind this would be our last night together." He released her shoulders and watched her as she sat up. "Were the twins very disappointed we didn't all have dinner together?"

"Yes, Jason, but we managed."

He walked to the door. "I guess it was a lousy ending to a beautiful two weeks."

"Yes, thanks to *you*," she said tightly.

"I don't think it's fair for you to be so angry and unforgiving," he said, "I should have been with you and the girls tonight, but as I told you before I hadn't realized this would be our last night together."

"I forgive you, Jason, as I have forgiven you so many times before."

He glared at her angrily and opened the door. "Good night, Lila," he said.

"Good night," she answered cooly. She lay in bed staring up at the ceiling and asked herself why it had upset her so that Jason and Nikki had gone out to dinner together that night. The answer came through to her all too clearly. She was jealous of Nikki, and that jealousy was caused by her love for Jason.

It had been several days since their return to Houston and Lila had seen very little of Jason. She could not determine whether he was deliberately avoiding her or not—she only knew the painful emptiness that she felt resulting from not being with him. She filled her days working with the twins and writing her book—activities that were no longer completely satisfying. Often she found herself longing to be in Jason's arms, to feel his warm possessive lips pressed to hers, but she knew their love was not meant to be. He was no doubt deeply involved with Nikki.

The telephone rang some five or six times before Lila picked up the receiver. Aunt Margaret, who had been back from Europe a week, was calling to invite her over on Thursday to view slides and snapshots of her trip. She asked Lila to invite Hunter to join them and to remind Ms. Katherine and Jason of the time and date. Lila accepted her aunt's invitation, agreed to carry out her requests and placed the receiver back in its cradle.

Reluctantly, she found Hunter's number in the telephone book and dialed it. She could not forget the coldness in his voice when last she spoke with him and vividly remembered promising herself she would never call him again. She also remembered that, for some unknown reason, Jason had forbidden her to contact Hunter, but she could see no way of getting around her aunt's request. She waited for him to answer the phone.

His voice came through the receiver amicably, but when Lila identified herself his tone changed. She told him the purpose of her call and awaited his answer. It was what she expected it to be, a polite "no, thank you." Lila hung up the phone annoyed with herself for feeling hurt and confused by his behavior.

She made up her mind to get all of her unpleasant tasks over with that evening, so she knocked on Jason's bedroom door. He opened it and hesitated momentarily. "Come in," he said, surprised but apparently pleased to see her standing there. She stepped into the room and her heart skipped a beat as her eyes involuntarily raked over his deeply tanned muscular, body clad only in a pair of white swim trunks, "I'm on my way to the pool. Join me?"

"No," she answered dryly.

"Have a seat," he offered.

"I'd rather stand."

"All right," he said and propped himself against a chest and waited for her to speak.

"I've only come to remind you that you're to be at Aunt Margaret's at 7:30 on Thursday."

"I hadn't forgotten."

"Good," she said and turned to leave the room.

He caught her arm. "Please, stay awhile." His voice was gentle and persuasive.

Lila knew she should leave his room but instead she asked, "Why?"

"I've missed you."

"When have you had time to miss me, Jason?" she asked. "You've been awfully busy with your work and Nikki, haven't you?"

"Yes. But I've missed you just the same."

"I see," she said and walked to one of the windows to look out.

"Mrs. Cobine brought up a pitcher of lemonade right before you came. Have some with me," he coaxed. She followed him over to his sitting room and sank into a huge leather chair.

"She knows I like a cool drink after my swim and was thoughtful enough to prepare this for me." He filled two glasses.

"Mrs. Cobine is very kind," Lila replied, not knowing what else to say.

Jason settled in a matching chair opposite her. "Let's not spend our time singing praises of Mrs. Cobine's virtue," he said. "Why have you been avoiding me?"

She looked at him wide eyed. "It's you who's been avoiding me," she corrected him.

He drank deeply from his glass. "No matter," he said, changing the subject, "go with me on Thursday to Aunt Margaret's."

"I'd planned to drive my own car."

"Plans are made to be broken," he said sarcastically.

"How original." She poured herself another glass of lemonade and maneuvered out of the spotlight. "Why have you turned Hunter against me, Jason?" she asked.

"What?" His eyes narrowed and his body grew tense.

"Twice I've called him and twice he has been just short of discourteous to me. That never happened before he met you. What have you said to him?"

"Why do you persist in hounding the man?" he asked angrily.

"I'm not hounding him," she said matter-of-factly. "Aunt Margaret asked me to invite him over on Thursday. I did and he declined. They have always enjoyed each other's company and now you've done or said something to turn him against both of us."

"Is it so important that he goes on Thursday?"

"Aunt Margaret will be disappointed if he doesn't."

"Then I'll see what I can do," he said, slamming his glass onto the table.

Lila was shocked by his words. "What kind of power do you have over him?" she asked.

"Don't concern yourself with Hunter," Jason replied evenly. She rose from her chair and walked to the door knowing somehow she would find out why Hunter's attitude had changed so drastically regarding their friendship. "You still haven't answered my question," Jason said. "Will you go with me to Aunt Margaret's on Thursday?"

"You haven't answered mine either," she retorted, "but I'll go with you on Thursday." She thought in some way her going with Jason would persuade him to give her more information about her friend.

"Good." He threw a towel over his shoulder. "Sure you won't join me for a swim?"

"Yes," she said, afraid of what would no doubt

happen if she went with him, but desiring his company all the same, "but I will join you in the library in an hour for a game of chess."

An arrogant smile pulled at Jason's lips as his eyes searched her face. "Terrific," he said, "see you then." He left for the pool and she went to her quarters.

After preparing her materials for the next morning's tutoring lessons, Lila slipped into a long terry lounging garment and brushed her hair to one side and tied it with a matching ribbon. The strapless magenta dress lifted her spirits and highlighted the rosiness of her complexion. She dabbed perfume onto her skin and went down to the library.

The chess table was in a far corner of the room and Lila went over and set the pieces and pawns in place for the game. She found a station on the radio that played jazz and adjusted the sound to a soft level. She picked up a magazine and began thumbing through it. The library door opened and Jason, in chocolate brown trousers and a loose fitting beige shirt, stepped into the room. His large dark eyes traveled immediately to her. "My favorite lady, my favorite music and my favorite game." He strolled over to the table. "What more can a man ask for?"

She smiled up at him, "How was your swim?"

"Good," he said, allowing his gaze to tarry on her bare shoulders.

"Shall we start the game?" she asked.

"If you insist." They moved the chessmen around the board skillfully and Lila presented quite a challenge for Jason, but after forty-five minutes the game was over and Jason emerged victorious.

"It was a good game," he complimented her.

"I enjoyed it," she said, getting up to stretch her legs. She walked across the room and sat on the sofa; Jason followed her.

"What now?" he asked with an amused expression on his face. She looked at him quizzically. "What's the real purpose of this cozy little set-up?"

"The purpose is for two friends to have an enjoyable evening together," she said. "I'm not devious like you, Jason."

"I see." He laughed heartily. "I think you've misjudged me. I've done nothing to warrant such an unsavory opinion of me."

"That's a matter of opinion."

"Yes. I guess it is." He reached over and played with her curls. "What can I do to change your view of my integrity?"

"Tell me what you've done to Hunter." Their eyes locked as Jason's large hand gripped her neck and pulled her to him.

"Nothing," he articulated. He got up from the sofa and stood over her. "Does the truth clear my name?"

"If what you just stated is the truth—no."

"I didn't think it would." He smiled and reached for her and she rose from the sofa. Ella Fitzgerald was singing softly to the music of Nelson Riddle. "A perfect ending to a lovely evening," he said, holding her close and guiding her expertly around the room. She felt comfortable in his arms and rested her head against his shoulder.

"What time on Thursday?" she asked.

"Seven." The music stopped and Jason walked her

to the foot of the stairs. He took her face in his hands and kissed her tender yielding mouth. "Good night." he said.

"Good night," she replied.

The next day was hectic for Lila. She overslept and this threw her regular routine off schedule. She skipped her morning swim, which always helped her day begin well, and had a quick breakfast, then tutored the girls. Since she had promised, she had to take them to their music lessons which limited her time for focusing her concentration on her morning writing. Nevertheless, after lunch, she drove them across town to the Whitehall School of Music and decided while they were having their lessons she would go to the branch library around the corner to check some dates for her book. To her dismay, the library did not have the information she needed and she would have to find time to go to the main building. She picked up the twins and drove back to the Tobias home in the evening rush-hour traffic. When they finally arrived, Lila's nerves were on edge and all she wanted to do was have her evening meal and relax in her room. She and the twins freshened up and went down to dinner. Lila entered the dining room and her heart sank, for sitting at the table with Jason and Aunt Katherine was Nikki Jocksay.

"I was worried you wouldn't make it back in time to have dinner with us," Aunt Katherine said. She looked at Lila closely. "What is it, my dear?" she asked. "You look so pale."

"I've had a very difficult day," Lila said, taking

her place at the table, wishing she *had* missed having dinner with them.

"You'll feel better after you've eaten," Aunt Katherine assured her. The meal was served and Lila ate and drank mechanically. Several attempts were made to include her in their conversation, but each effort was futile. Lila resented having to sit at the same table with Nikki, but realized Jason could invite whomever he pleased to his home for dinner. She was aware she was being grossly impolite and tried to smile and be pleasant, but couldn't hide her hostility. She excused herself and left the room.

A light breeze was ciruclating in the patio and Lila reclined in one of the lounge chairs, attempting to sort out her thoughts when Aunt Katherine's voice startled her. "Are you feeling better?" she asked.

"I'm much better," Lila said, "and I'm sorry if I spoiled dinner for you."

"You needn't apologize for anything," the older woman said. "Sometimes certain situations are difficult to take." She smiled and patted her shoulder knowingly. They sat quietly enjoying the evening together and after a while they retired for the night.

At seven o'clock Thursday evening Lila waited for Jason in the library. "Right on time," he said entering the room, "shall we leave?" They got into the car and headed west across town.

"Isn't Aunt Katherine riding with us?" Lila asked.

"No. She left in her car directly after dinner. I think she wanted to help Aunt Margaret prepare things."

"I see," Lila said, "I could have helped also."

"They want this to be their special little production," Jason replied. "Did you bring our Cancun pictures?"

"Yes. Aunt Katherine reminded me to bring them this morning. I hope we don't bore everyone too much with our vacations."

"I doubt it," Jason said.

They rode for a period in silence before Lila asked, "Where's Nikki this evening?"

"I don't know."

She smiled at him sweetly.

"Again the truth throws a shadow over my character," he said looking at her briefly and smiling. She did not audibly reply but agreed with him silently.

The mood was festive when Lila and Jason entered Aunt Margaret's condominium. She walked over to kiss her aunt hello and was interrupted by Hunter. "Good evening, Lila." He spoke formally.

"Hello." She was pleased to see him and wondered what Jason had done to get him to change his mind. "How have you been?" she asked earnestly concerned about him.

"Very well."

"I'm glad to see you," she said sincerely, "Aunt Margaret would have been very disappointed had you not come."

"I know," he replied.

She looked around for Jason and saw that he was watching them. "Excuse me," she said, "I must speak to Aunt Margaret. Perhaps we'll have an opportunity to talk some before you leave." She looked at him expectantly.

"Perhaps."

She spoke to her aunt and some of the other guests. Then for lack of anything better to do while she thought of a way to best approach Hunter again, she picked up one of the delicious looking sandwiches arranged on a silver tray and poured herself some wine.

"Well, are you pleased?" Jason asked, taking her glass from her and drinking from it.

"I'd just like to know what you said to him," she said filling another glass. He smiled at her and walked away.

"All right everybody," her aunt announced. "We're ready to show the slides. Their guests took seats on chairs, sofas and the floor and Aunt Margaret and Aunt Katherine commented on the pictures as they were flashed on the screen. It was obvious the septuagenarians had had a wonderful trip and when they finished showing their slides everyone applauded. Questions were asked and conversations resumed and Lila looked around for Hunter. He was deep in conversation with Aunt Margaret when she spotted him, and by the time she made her way over to them Hunter was moving quite swiftly toward the door.

"Here are some pictures that Lila and Jason took when they were in Cancun a few weeks ago with the twins," Aunt Katherine said. Someone took the pictures and began passing them around the room.

"You weren't even going to say good-bye," Lila said, managing to get to the door before he could open it. She looked hurt.

"I didn't want to disturb you," he said.

"Won't you stay a little longer?"

"I have another engagement," he said curtly. "We'll talk some other time, Lila."

She stood back and allowed him to open the door. "Good-bye Hunter," she said and turned to go back to the party. Jason was standing in the doorway of the living room and she realized that again he had been watching them.

Chapter Seven

The mid-August day inspired Lila to do little more than stretch out in the shade of an oak tree and thumb through a fashion magazine. After giving the girls their morning lessons, she had taken her manuscript to the post office and mailed it to her editor. She was thrilled that at last her book was completed and looked forward to a few days rest before starting her next one. She put her magazine aside and slipped into the pool, swimming slowly across it on her back. It wasn't long however before she climbed out and toweled herself dry. The noon day sun was too hot to remain in the water. Hunger pains motivated her into the kitchen still clad in her purple and green bikini to make a sandwich and a cold drink. The house was quiet. Mr. and Mrs. Cobine were away on holiday and Aunt Katherine had taken the twins to lunch and a movie. Lila was in the house alone. Lazily she sliced roast beef, tomatoes and onions, placed them on a piece of dark bread, sprinkled salt and pepper on top and covered it with a lettuce leaf and a second slice of bread smeared with mayonnaise and mustard. She filled a glass with ice and poured fruit juice over it, grabbed a couple of paper napkins and headed for the patio.

"My, my, how the cook has changed," Jason said, coming into the kitchen loosening his tie. His eyes ran over Lila casually. "I'd like to have one of the same," he said, looking at her plate. Lila had not seen him for several days and could not fathom why he was home midday on a Tuesday.

"Are you serious about the sandwich?" she asked.

"I'd love one as soon as I change out of these hot clothes." She made a sandwich and a cold drink for Jason and took their plates and glasses out to the patio. Within minutes, Jason, wearing his swim trunks, joined her. "Do I get the cook for dessert?" he asked taking a bite out of his sandwich and smiling mischievously. "This is delicious," he added.

"Thank you," Lila replied watching him devour the sandwich hungrily, "and no you don't get the cook for dessert," she countered playfully. "What are you doing home this time of day?"

"I decided to give myself the afternoon off," he said.

For the first time that afternoon he seemed to have realized Lila was not sequestered in her rooms writing. "Why aren't you at the typewriter?" he asked.

"I'm giving myself the day off, too." She smiled proudly. "I completed my book and mailed it today."

"Congratulations," Jason said looking at her surprised. "Does that mean that now we'll see more of you?"

"For a couple of days," she said suspecting that Jason didn't really care whether or not she had free time. "After that I start on the outline for my next book."

"I admire your talent," he said offhandedly.

His compliment was unexpected and Lila turned from him fearful he might detect how much it meant to her. "Thank you," she managed to say coolly. "It's a relief knowing I've completed one of my major projects for the summer," she added, "and that the next one will be completed in three weeks."

"What happens then?"

"I'll find a place of my own and continue my writing."

For a moment his eyes held hers. "Don't leave us, Lila," he said softly.

"The twins will be fine," she said quickly, growing a bit uneasy with his intimate tone. "They take their tests the end of this week and I'm confident they'll do well."

"I see," he said getting up from his chair. "We've

been fortunate having you with us this summer." His eyes sought hers but she avoided his gaze. "I hope the experience has been at least half as rewarding for you as it has been for us."

"It has been," she said.

He gave her a sidelong glance. "Only half?" he asked teasingly.

"Oh, Jason." She laughed lightly. "Working with the twins this summer has been one of the most fulfilling experiences of my life." She watched him as he walked back to his chair and sat down, stretching lazily but gracefully catlike and looking into the distance.

"Are the twins the only ones in this family that have made a difference in your life?" His question was meant to goad her into commenting on their personal relationship, however she flatly refused to accommodate him.

"Aunt Katherine will always be very dear to me," she said, attempting to answer his question without exposing her Achilles heel, "and I will always be grateful for the kindnesses and friendship of Mr. and Mrs. Cobine."

Jason's smile was slow and sardonic; his tone was cold. "I think you've covered everyone in the house for the exception of Cherries and me."

Before she realized it she had said, "Oh, I'll miss Cherries." Jason's eyes clung to her and she blushed crimson.

"Yes. I'm sure you will." Again he rose from his chair and began pacing in front of her.

Lila could feel the tension building between them and was uncomfortable with it. She wanted to clear the air but not at her own expense, so she tried to change the subject. "What are you doing tonight?" she asked.

"Why? Are you asking me for a date?"

"Yes," she answered, not having anything in mind when she asked the question. He waited for her to continue. "I had planned to go ice skating tonight," she lied. "I'd like your company."

He eyed her keenly. "I haven't skated in years."

"I haven't either," she said. "It should be fun." She was relieved that she had managed to divert his attention away from questioning her about the summer. She was not up to talking with him about their relationship. She picked up their dishes and started toward the kitchen.

"What time are you picking me up?" he asked.

"Around eight?" she answered, surprised he had taken her up on her offer.

"Good. See you then." He walked to the pool and before she could get their plates and glasses in the kitchen she heard him dive in.

The ice skating rink was moderately crowded when Jason and Lila arrived. They pulled on skates and stepped out onto the ice and for the first few minutes they were both a little shaky. But after a few strides—close to the rail for support—they were gliding smoothly and confidently around the rink.

Lila tried a few jumps and spins and found herself accepting Jason's help up from the ice in quite a few instances. Her skating skills were indeed rusty. Jason, however, was able to impressively execute a few difficult maneuvers that he had not attempted since high school days. They laughed a lot as they gamboled along together. Occasionally Jason would lift Lila and skate with her in his arms and she would cling to him for support. She wished they could always get along so well together but immediately remembered two reasons why it was so difficult—Hunter Matthews and Nikki Jocksay. She was disturbed by his relationship with both of them.

An announcement was made for the skaters to clear the ice for resurfacing and Lila and Jason—having skated for a couple of hours—decided to leave. "It was a surprisingly fun evening," he said to her as they climbed into the MG.

"You're a good skater." She drove along South Post Oak to San Felipe, made a left turn and drove several more blocks before parking in front of a new condominium complex.

"Are you kidnapping me?" Jason asked looking about not understanding why she had taken him there.

"No, of course not," she answered enjoying his playful mood. "I'd like your opinion of the place."

"Why, are you planning to buy the building?"

"Not all of it." Her reply alerted him to her intentions and his displeasure with her decision was conveyed in his acid reply.

"It's not for you, Lila," he answered after a moment. His mood had changed.

"Jason, I'll need a place in three weeks and I don't like making such a serious decision by myself. I'm earnestly asking for your opinion."

"You have a home, Lila."

"No. I don't have a home," she said softly, "and if

you refuse to help me make a sound choice in buying a place, I'll do it alone."

"I'll never help you." His anger was bitter and for the first time since she had moved back to Houston Lila felt desperately alone. She started the MG and headed toward Caroline Street fighting back the tears that strained to flow from her eyes.

Lila stood at the window looking out at the pool. It had been difficult for her to sleep after the tense ride home with Jason. She glanced at the clock, 3:30 A.M. Although she couldn't understand why he wanted her to remain in his home, she knew that moving out would be the only sensible thing for her to do. She resolved to look for a place each day after her tutoring sessions with Daisy and Violet until she found something that she liked and could afford. She would have to find something by the end of three weeks. She couldn't live in Jason's house a day longer than that. With that resolution firmly fixed in her mind she pulled on her swimsuit and made her way quietly out to the pool.

The moon was full and the night was clear and warm. Lila slipped into the water and was momentarily winded by its coldness. She swam the length several times before becoming aware of eyes watching her. Her body grew tense as she moved to the side to pull herself out and saw Cherries curled up in a lounge chair looking in her direction. She chuckled softly to herself and went over and took him in her arms. "You scared me," she said, stroking him and walking back to the side of the pool. She sat down with her legs folded under her and continued to talk to the little dog. Soon, however, the eerie feeling that a pair of eyes were on her returned. Cherries wiggled from her arms and she watched him run toward the shadows. His bark was friendly which told Lila nothing. Cherries liked everybody. She sat still, afraid to move and called softly for the little dog to come back to her. When he didn't she got to her feet and dashed for the house. She stopped in her tracks, however, when a figure directly in front of her moved across the patio and disappeared around the corner of the house. After a brief scuffling in the darkness, Jason—with Cherries in his arms—emerged.

"I'm so glad it's you," Lila said rushing to him.

"Get in the house quickly," he replied walking fast behind her. He put Cherries down and locked the door. "What were you doing out there this time of morning by yourself?" he demanded.

"I couldn't sleep so I went for a swim," she said unsteadily.

"At this time of morning by yourself?"

"You do it all the time, Jason," she said, her mood changing. "Why can't I?"

"Obviously because you're not capable of taking care of yourself." They glared at each other before Lila turned away from him and walked into the kitchen. "It was lucky I came out when I did," he said. "You could have been hurt. Please don't ever go out at night alone again." He followed her visibly attempting to control his anger.

Lila sat at the kitchen counter and rested her head in her hands. "All right," she conceded, slowly recognizing the genuine concern in his voice and eyes. "What happened out there?" She raised her head to look at him. "Are you hurt?"

"No. I'm fine." He sat down beside her. "Someone was trying to take Cherries. We struggled a little but he got away. There's been quite a bit of dognapping in this neighborhood lately."

"Dognapping? Why?"

"Dog fights," Jason said. "A lot of it goes on outside Houston and dogs like Cherries are used to train fighting dogs."

"That's awful," Lila said shivering. "I never would have allowed Cherries to follow me outside if I had known he would be in danger."

"I know, but it's all over now. Maybe you should try and get some sleep."

"I'm more awake now than ever," she said, thinking of what could have happened.

"I have the perfect solution for that," Jason walked over to the cupboard.

"A swim?" Lila asked sarcastically.

"Not for you." His gaze held hers. "A cup of herb tea will do the trick just as well. Get into some dry clothes and meet me in the library."

Lila changed into a pair of green cotton lounging pajamas and went back downstairs to the library. Jason had a pot of hot tea on the table. He poured a cup and handed it to her as she settled herself on the sofa. "Did you call the police?" she asked.

"Yes. They promised to investigate."

The tea felt good as it trickled down Lila's throat. She emptied her cup and felt the hot liquid warm and relax her insides. She allowed Jason to pour more tea for her and watched him as he sat down beside her. Lila had grown to enjoy the warm homey library and felt especially comfortable relaxing on the sofa next to Jason. It all made her feel a little sad, however, for in three weeks she would no longer be able to enjoy its coziness.

"Feeling better?" Jason asked, scrutinizing her so closely that she was almost sure he had read her thoughts.

"Much better," she replied forcing a smile.

"You're preoccupied," he observed.

She couldn't avoid his dark piercing eyes and attempted to speak off-handedly. "I was just thinking that you were right about the tea. I'm beginning to feel drowsy."

"Good," Jason said, encouraging her to rest her head on his shoulder. The rhythm of his breathing and the thumping of his heartbeat helped to lull her to sleep. After a while he lifted her in his arms and carried her upstairs. She was aware of him gently laying her on the bed, intently staring down at her a few minutes before abruptly turning and leaving the room.

It had been ten days since the twins had taken their exams at Smith Academy and now they anxiously waited for their uncle to open the letter that would give them their test results. When his lips pulled into a broad smile and he read that they had been accepted at the academy they had all rejoiced. Lila was particularly happy that the girls had made such high scores in reading and math and was confident they would have a successful school year.

"It's been a wonderful summer," Aunt Katherine

said as they took their places at the dinner table. "Thanks to you Lila, my dear."

"Daisy and Violet were excellent students," Lila said, feeling that Aunt Katherine's laudatory remarks should be shared with the girls, "if they hadn't been enthusiastic and hard-working nothing I could have done would have been successful. They deserve all the praise."

"Of course they do," their great-aunt said, "and I'm very proud of them." The twins beamed as the attention was shifted to them and they wanted to know what they would do to celebrate their big accomplishment.

"Yes. Let's celebrate," Jason said. "What would you two like to do?"

The girls thought for a moment before they decided they would enjoy a swim party in the backyard with their friends. Jason agreed with their idea and suggested the party be held the following evening. Aunt Katherine and Lila volunteered to help with preparations and supervision and after dinner they worked out the details.

At five o'clock the next evening the boys and girls that had been invited to the party arrived. They followed Daisy and Violet out to the pool and immediately became involved in a game of tag. They played for a while and then Jason got in the pool with them and organized two race teams promising prizes for the winning team. The children took to the idea and within minutes the race was under way. Lila watched Jason as he supervised them giving the weaker swimmers a little help, but rooting for all of the children. His face was vibrant and alive and it was obvious he was enjoying himself. Lila thought how lucky Violet and Daisy were to have Jason as their guardian. It was clear that he loved them very much. He happily gave them so much of his time. Lila knew he also loved his aunt and wished he could find space in his heart to include her; however, in a few days she would be leaving this happy little family and the thought made her sad.

"This team is the winner," she heard Jason say and the children cheered for themselves. "Ms. Lila would you please bring the medals for our best swimmers."

Lila and Ms. Katherine had planned several different kinds of games for the children to compete in and Jason had been thoughtful enough to buy prizes for them. Lila could see that this idea would be well appreciated. She took the silver-colored medals to Jason and he gave one to each child on the winning team. "And now bring the medals for our second-place winners," he announced, and the losing team cheered for itself. Bronze-colored medals were given to them and the children pinned the medals on their swimsuits and jumped in the pool and resumed their play.

Jason and Lila set out grilled hot dogs and trimmings on a table and called the children to eat. After they had completed their meal, Jason organized a game of horseshoes and displayed a large stuffed teddy bear dressed in football gear for the winner. Volleyball was played and enjoyed and then the children went back in the pool and played until their parents picked them up.

"It was a wonderful party," Violet said to her uncle as she helped take some of the dishes into the kitchen.

"Yes, it was great," Daisy added. "Thanks for letting us have it."

"I enjoyed the party too, girls," Jason said.

"Lila and Aunt Katherine thought of some good games for us to play," they observed. "The volleyball game was fun."

"Yes, they did," Jason replied, "and it's too bad Lila is going away soon and won't be here to help us plan parties in the future."

"Going away?" the girls asked, surprised by their uncle's statement. "What do you mean?"

"Lila plans to move in a few days," Jason informed them.

"But she can't do that," Daisy said with tears in her eyes, "we're a family and people don't move away from their family." They looked at him disbelievingly.

"What's the matter, girls?" Aunt Katherine asked, coming in from the backyard and noticing the stress on the girls' faces.

"Uncle Jason says Lila is moving away soon," they said, and ran to their aunt for comfort. She put an arm around each girl and they all looked to Jason for the answer.

"Why would she want to do that?" Aunt Katherine asked. "I thought she was happy here with us." Lila came into the kitchen with the horseshoes and volleyball and Cherries at her heels.

"That does it," she said. "Everything has been cleared away and the yard is as good as new." She turned to smile at the girls and was taken aback by the four pairs of eyes boring into her. "What is it?" she asked. Lila could not imagine what she had done to cause them to look at her distressfully. She drew in her breath slowly and asked again, "What is it?"

Jason walked across the room and sat at the small breakfast table with Aunt Katherine and the girls and pulled out a chair indicating that she should join them. Lila placed the volleyball and horseshoes on the kitchen counter and took her place at the table with the rest of the family. She looked from one to the other until Jason decided to speak.

"I've told them that you plan to leave us in a few days," Jason said. "It's difficult for them to understand why you can't remain here." Lila's heart sank as she met the twins' gaze and she tried hard to think of a way to explain her need for leaving to the little girls. She realized Jason had used them in his ploy to get her to stay and fought back the anger that this realization aroused in her. She looked at her hands, which were clasped together resting on the table, and swallowed hard to alleviate the dryness that had suddenly come in her throat. She couldn't bear hurting the twins, but even more she couldn't remain in Jason's house.

"We all agreed I would tutor you girls for the three summer months," Lila said, attempting to make her explanation as simple as possible. "I've stuck to that agreement. You've accomplished the goal that I was hired to help you to accomplish and summer will be over in a few days. It's time for me to go."

"But you don't have to leave," Violet said. "We

love you, Lila. You're part of the family. Please stay."

The child's plea was so earnest and heart warming Lila had to press her lips together tightly to keep herself from weeping. Aunt Katherine realized Lila was having a problem consoling the little girls and so she spoke on her behalf.

"Let's give Lila a chance to think over our offer to remain here with us," she said to Violet and Daisy. "Perhaps after she has had a chance to think awhile she'll change her mind." Her eyes searched Lila's face. "But if she doesn't, we'll have to accept her decision and realize how fortunate we've been that Lila shared her life with us this summer."

Lila was grateful for Aunt Katherine's intervention and managed to smile at the two worried little faces that weakly smiled back at her.

"Now it's time for bed," Aunt Katherine continued. "Give Lila and Jason a big hug and kiss and I'll do the honors of tucking you in tonight." The girls obeyed their great-aunt and the three of them left the kitchen. Jason and Lila remained sitting at the table.

"I hope you'll do as Aunt Katherine suggested and reconsider our offer," Jason said finally. "You'll make two little girls very happy."

"I'm sure I would," Lila said, getting up from the table, "but I doubt seriously if I'll change my mind." She walked out into the hall and Jason followed her. "It was unfair of you to upset the girls that way," she said, no longer angry with him.

"It's only right they know you plan to leave in a few days," he said. "And don't forget, you've led

them to believe you'll at least think about staying."
He stopped her at the foot of the stairs and took her
in his arms.

Lila did not resist his embrace. "I'll keep my
promise," she said coolly.

"Good." His lips sought hers and his kiss was long
and tender. Lila clung to him and returned it with
the same warmth and gentleness to his surprise and
pleasure. Afterward, she pulled away from him and
went up to bed.

Lila had spent the morning looking at condominiums and townhouses and had found nothing she
both liked and could afford. Although she had kept
her promise and thought about staying on at the
Tobias home, her conclusion had been the same. She
would move as soon as she found a suitable place.
Remaining in the same house with the wayward
Jason Tobias would cause her too much heartache.

Feeling despondent after her disappointing morning, Lila drove over to the Galleria Shopping Center
to treat herself to a shopping spree. There was
nothing that she really needed or wanted, but she
knew that once inside the shops she would find
something to buy that would lift her spirits. She
began her browsing in one of the exclusive jewelry
stores looking at rings and watches. She moved
around the counter and allowed her eyes to search a
display of gold bracelets. A heavy chain link one
caught her eye and she asked to try it on. The
bracelet looked lovely on her arm and so she bought
it. She walked slowly through the airconditioned
mall looking in the shop windows, finally coming to

one of her favorite stores, Lord & Taylor. Lila stopped at the cosmetic counter and smelled a couple of the perfumes. She liked one with a delicate flowery fragrance and bought not only the perfume but also the soap, dusting powder and body lotion. With these purchases she took a leisurely walk back toward the parking area. A white dress in a small dress shop caught her eye and she went in to take a closer look at it. She found several others on the rack that she liked and decided to try them on, after which she felt compelled to buy two of them. She decided she might as well buy shoes to go with the dresses so she walked across the way to a shoe store and found a couple of pairs that she liked. She purchased them too then made her way to her car and back to the Tobias home.

Her mind drifted to Jason and her relationship with him as she drove. They had had some wonderful times together over the summer and she knew it would be impossible for her to ever forget him. She pondered over their many arguments and disagreements and realized that at the crux of most of them were his dubious relationships with Nikki and Hunter. Although she longed to be the object of his affections, she realized he was not worth the heartache he would surely cause her if she allowed her love for him to grow. He was much too capricious and Lila knew that she could not tolerate a wayward lover. She knew she had to push the handsome and unpredictable Jason Tobias out of her mind.

When she arrived at the house she found her Aunt Margaret there visiting Ms. Katherine. "You've been shopping," her aunt observed, when Lila walked into the living room with her bags and boxes in her arms.

"Yes, I have," she replied happily, "I've just treated myself to a marvelous shopping spree at the Galleria. Come up and see what I've bought."

The two ladies followed her up to her rooms and watched as she unwrapped her packages. They ooohed and aaahed over the lovely gold bracelet, the silk dresses, leather shoes and the delicate fragrance of the perfume. "When and where do you plan to wear all of these beautiful things?" asked Aunt Margaret.

It had never occurred to Lila that she should want to do something special in her new purchases. She thought for a moment before she answered, "Out to dinner tonight. I think I'll try to get reservations at Tony's." She went to the phone and dialed the number. "Come with me?" she invited them.

Aunt Katherine and Aunt Margaret exchanged worried glances. "Are you sure you'd like the company of two old ladies, my dear," Aunt Katherine asked.

"Yes, of course," Lila answered holding her hand over the mouth of the receiver. "They have a table for three," she informed them. "Please come with me."

"We'd love to, Lila," said her aunt. They watched her as she finished her conversation and hung up. "But are you sure you wouldn't rather invite some nice young man?" she asked.

"Positive," Lila answered flatly. She realized they were perplexed by her actions, but she was not up to explaining to them that she had no nice young man to invite and was in no mood to spend the evening in her rooms alone. They agreed to be ready for seven and left her to rest.

Lila awoke from her nap feeling refreshed and ready for the evening out with Aunts Margaret and Katherine. She took a long hot bath with her new perfumed soap and afterward dabbed some of the new fragrance onto her skin. She slipped into the gray and peach silk jersey dress and gray high-heeled sandals that she had bought earlier and brushed her hair until the loose bouncy curls gleamed. She took a small gray colored leather handbag from the drawer, placed her necessary items in it and left her room. The aunts were ready and waiting for her when she entered the library and Aunt Katherine volunteered to drive them to the restaurant in her orange BMW.

Tony's, located on South Post Oak, was one of the most elegant and luxurious restaurants in Houston. Its dark wood paneling, tasteful paintings and arrangements of fresh flowers provided just the sophisticated atmosphere that Lila was in the mood for. They arrived in a convivial mood and were immediately taken to their table. Their waiter, dressed in black tie, came to take their order. For an appetizer Lila and Aunt Margaret had oysters Rockefeller and Aunt Katherine ordered a crab crepé. The aunts then ordered trout Veronique, which was fresh trout with white grapes in a delicate white wine sauce for an entree and Lila chose the frog legs with wild rice. Their meal was superb and they enjoyed it, amusing each other with happy and interesting anecdotes. Their table was cleared and the waiter took their order for dessert, three chocolate soufflés. While they waited for their desserts they looked around the room at ladies in designer gowns and chafing dishes aflame.

"I've always liked this place," said Lila happily. "I'm glad we came."

"I am too dear," Aunt Katherine replied.

"Yes, it's my kind of restaurant," added Aunt Margaret. "Thank you for inviting us, Lila."

"The pleasure is all mine," the young woman said, watching the waiter as he approached their table and set their desserts before them. She took a spoonful of the soufflé and smiled appreciatively, "It's delicious," she said.

She looked up at the aunts whose faces were now pale and whose eyes lingered on the entrance of the room. Lila turned to follow their gaze and looked squarely into the faces of a party of four waiting to be seated. Jason with Nikki holding on to his arm tightly, and Hunter and a very attractive woman spotted them and immediately came over to their table, exchanged greetings and Hunter introduced the redhead as Sarah—his wife. The foursome, obviously out to celebrate a special occasion, were then led to their table leaving Lila and the aunts to finish their desserts. The festive mood of the three remaining at the table ceased and they quickly paid their bill and left the restaurant. The drive home was very long and quiet.

A smile lingered on Lila's lips after she had completed her telephone conversation. The wonderful news from her editor was just what she needed on this gray late summer morning. The publishing house was very excited about her book and anticipated it selling well. Her novel, *Winter's Revenge*, would be in the book stores the first of the year and Lila looked forward to seeing her work in print. She happily pulled on a pair of khaki slacks and a white T shirt and went out to find herself a place to live.

Chapter Eight

Lila left the house, although Ms. Katherine had warned her that inclement weather was expected. A flash flood watch had been issued over the radio and TV and heavy clouds hung dark and threatening overhead. Lila decided, however, to take a chance and try to beat the rain. She convinced herself she could make it to a couple of places before the rain began so she hurriedly climbed into her car and drove away. She had not gotten very far when large drops of rain started to fall, but because she was so determined to find herself someplace to live she continued her drive out to West Belt. She turned the car radio on and again it was announced that flash floods were imminent. Lila ignored the threat of the devastating rains and continued her drive. She arrived at the Pinevill Garden Condominium in heavy rain and grabbed her umbrella and went into the sales office. A small friendly man greeted her at the door and introduced himself as John the sales representative. He expressed his surprise that she had come to see a condominium in such severe weather and informed her that a flash flood warning was now in effect. Lila, disregarded the sales representative's warning and explained to him what she was looking for and her price range. He gave her a brochure and promised to show her one of the models as soon as the rain stopped. He then offered her a cup of tea while she waited, which she gladly accepted. They talked for about thirty minutes; however, the rain did not let up and John agreed to take Lila to see the model that she was interested in. The two bedroom condominium that she chose to see had beautiful custom-built solid ash cabinets, marble vanities and full carpeting in the bath. The bricked kitchen was complete with a self-cleaning oven, dishwasher and trash compactor. In addition to a formal living and dinning rooms, there was a spacious breakfast nook and garden room. After thoroughly inspecting the condominium, Lila decided it was too large for her and instead of going back to the sales office with John she dashed for her car.

It had been raining steadily for more than an hour when Lila pulled away from the curb on West Belt. She had planned to look at townhouses on Memorial Drive so she drove east and then north. Some streets she had wanted to travel were flooded, and she was forced to continually change her route. She successfully followed several cars down the middle of a street that was flooded which enabled her to turn onto Memorial Drive. She drove until she came to Cartson on Memorial, a new townhouse community that she had read about in the paper. She was anxious to examine its greenhouse baths and two-story skylit rooms, but when she arrived at the sales office she found the sales personnel preparing to leave.

"We're closing now," one of them said to her as he hurriedly locked the door. "We don't want to have to stay here in the office tonight. Come back tomorrow."

He ran to his car and pulled away leaving Lila standing in the downpour. Angry that the sales people had been so rude, she climbed back into her car and started for home. She realized several inches of rain had fallen on the city over a short period of time and it seemed as if there would be no immediate end to it. It was then that she began to remember why the rain had caused everyone to become so jittery. Slowly she approached an intersection that was flooded and attempted to cross it behind another car but midway the MG stalled. Lila tried to start it again but to no avail. She sat looking about her trying to determine what she should do next and suddenly realized water was lapping about her ankles. Her heart began to pound wildly and ironically a smile tugged at her lips. Now she understood quite clearly why the rain had caused everyone to become so tense and strained.

Although the rain had slacked some, water was rapidly seeping into the MG. Lila, growing more frightened, got out of the car and scrambled onto its hood. The streets had suddenly become rivers and more and more cars stalled sending their occupants to find refuge on their tops. As far as the eye could see, water had moved in and taken up residence where streets, sidewalks and pathways had once prevailed. Lila smiled weakly and waved back at a couple sitting atop a green sedan. It was interesting that some were maintaining a sense of humor, Lila could not. The water was now creeping over the hood of the MG and it was just a matter of time before it would completely cover it.

She looked around, searching the area carefully, to see if there was someplace where she could find shelter and realized not only had the rain become heavier than before but the winds were now gusty. The MG began to rock beneath her and she felt herself slipping into the water. She frantically tried to maintain her balance but found herself in water waist deep.

"Swim over here," the friendly couple, who had waved at her earlier, called to her and she made her way over to the top of the green sedan. They helped her up and they all tenaciously clung to the roof of the car.

The rain continued to come down steadily and the complete submergence of larger vehicles was imminent. Lila closed her eyes to shut out the fearful sight around her, but a soft roar approaching them forced her to look in its direction.

A man in a motorboat was coming toward them and Lila along with her companions thanked him profusely as he came alongside the car and without invitation from their rescuer they climbed aboard his boat. The man took them to higher ground where they were able to wade to safety.

Several boats were out now rescuing stranded motorists and small domestic animals. Some boatsmen, however, were loaded to capacity with household items. Their homes had either been flooded or they expected the high waters to reach them within a matter of minutes.

Lila stood on the sidewalk with no purse or other personal belongings—they had been lost somewhere along the way. "What will you do now?" she was asked by the man of the friendly couple.

"I don't know," she said, tucking her wet hair behind her ears. "Somehow I've managed to lose my purse and now I have no money. I can't even make a phone call. Looks like I'll have to walk home."

"What direction?" he asked.

"East—to Caroline Street."

"We're going in the same direction," he said, "we might as well walk together."

"Good," Lila replied, "I'd like some company."

The rain now fell gently and steadily as they attempted to make their way to a major thoroughfare. They encountered many flooded streets, however, which forced them to make several long detours. But, finally, they made their way to San Felipe Street and joined several others milling about the sidewalk and curb who were seeking refuge from their flooded out cars and homes. They chatted with one or two of the people in the group who informed them that to travel any distance either east or south they would have to wade in water at least knee deep. The idea of not knowing where or what she was stepping on disoriented Lila earlier and she did not relish the idea of having that experience again. However, she also did not like the idea of standing idly on the streets and so she decided to continue her journey. But just as she was about to walk away, a young man in a gray van drove up and offered a ride to anyone who was going as far as South Post Oak and Alabama Avenue.

Lila and several others decided to accept his offer and climbed into the van. She waved goodbye to the couple—they would walk to a friend's house close by—and gazed solemnly out of the window. She thought of her MG, completely covered by water, and wondered about the cost of having it repaired. She would no doubt have to buy a new car—a fact that did not lift her spirits. She would also have to replace her credit cards and driver's license; she wished she had been able to hold on to her purse, but it had been impossible. With effort, she pushed those problems from her thoughts and immediately her mind drifted to her Aunt Margaret and the Tobias family. She hoped they had survived the flood with no losses or serious incidents. She realized now she should have listened to Aunt Katherine and not gone out in such severe weather, but she had allowed her emotions instead of her good judgement to dictate her actions.

Lila could hear water gurgling beneath the van as it moved slowly through a stretch of deep water. The young driver quickly turned his radio up to distract his riders' attention away from the awesome sound. The current weather conditions were being announced and the citizens were warned not to attempt to travel the flooded streets unless it was absolutely necessary. Some lives had been lost in the flood and property damage so far had been estimated in the range of several million dollars.

Lila, along with the other passengers, thanked the young driver when they arrived at their destination. With the weatherman's warning fresh on her mind, she decided to try and find someplace to stay for a while and not continue her efforts to make it back home. She looked about her and realized she was in the vicinity of three hotels and decided to go to one and sit in the lobby until conditions improved. She made her way to the Houston Oaks Hotel and instead of stopping in the lobby, which was crowded with people, as she had planned she followed a motley group up on the elevator and found herself atop the hotel in the Galleria Roof. The nightclub overlooked southwest Houston giving its patrons an expansive view of the area, but tonight no one seemed interested in the view. People were laughing, talking and ordering drinks as if they were celebrating the end of a perfect day instead of waiting for the proper moment to face the ordeal that the weather presented. Lila stood close by the door unable to move any farther into the room. Waiters moved among the crowd taking orders for drinks. When one reached Lila to take her order she asked to use the telephone. He directed her to a phone she could use without cost and she tried to contact both Aunts Margaret and Katherine but their phones were out of order. She wandered back into the smoke filled room and leaned against a wall surveying the crowd. A short, stout gentleman approached her and offered to buy her a drink. Lila accepted an iced tea which the man, who had introduced himself as Samuel Jones, happily ordered for her. He then led her over to a table where several others were sitting and introduced her as Lila a fellow stranded citizen. It was a congenial group and for the first time in several hours Lila began to relax. Nevertheless, it was now early evening and she could not help but wonder when and how she would ever get home.

From the moment she had insisted on leaving that morning Aunt Katherine, Mr. and Mrs. Cobine and the twins had worried about Lila being caught in the flood. They realized she had been very upset and not thinking clearly when she left and hoped she would be able to cope with the flood conditions when she ran into them.

When Jason arrived home that evening and learned Lila had been out since late morning and no one had heard from her since that time, he became worried. He tried to call Aunt Margaret, but her phone was out of order. He then questioned the family as to what Lila's plans had been and then went out to look for her.

The newspaper that Lila had used earlier to find suitable living quarters had been marked and left in the library and Jason used it as a guide for his search.

Several places in various areas of the city had been circled and Jason, thinking Lila would attempt to drive only a short distance in such threatening weather, began his search in the closest area, the southeast. He attempted to reach Clayburn Village by driving due east, but the numerous stalled cars and unfamiliar streets flooded with water forced him to change his course. Finally, he was able to get within two blocks of the complex. He parked his car on a side street and began walking the distance to the townhouses. "Hey, mister," a youngster called to him, "are you going to Clayburn Village?" Jason turned and looked in the face of a boy who appeared to be about fifteen years old.

"Yes," he answered.

"Mind if I walk along with you?" the boy asked.

"No," Jason replied. "Do you live around here?"

"Yes, I live in one of the townhouses." They walked along the sidewalk that was gradually sloping into water. "It's safer to cross here and walk down the middle of the street," the boy said, indicating with a stick the path they should take.

"Sounds like you've done this before," Jason said.

"Yeah, I have," the boy replied. "I helped my

mom and little sister to safety about an hour ago. Most of the people who live in these houses left about that time." They were slowly moving into deeper water as they neared the community.

"Why are you going back?" Jason asked.

The boy smiled shyly. "To get my little sister's kitten," he said. "She's worried about him."

"You must love your sister very much," Jason said eyeing the boy.

"She's a sweet kid," he replied embarrassed. They moved into water above their knees as they laboriously groped for the curb in front of the townhouse community. "Which house is yours," the boy asked.

"Oh, I don't live here." They pulled themselves up on a grassy knoll. "The people here have been very lucky. None of the houses seem to be damaged."

"Yes, we have been lucky," the youngster replied. "But the bayou is swelling awfully fast and if it should overflow we may have problems."

"I hope that doesn't happen," Jason said. "Where's the sales office?"

The boy looked at him quizzically. "You came to buy a house in a flood?" His young face registered disbelief and Jason laughed softly. "No," he said. "I'm looking for a very dear friend of mine. She may have come here earlier and gotten stranded."

"Oh," the boy said, "it's the last building to your left."

Jason went to the sales office but no one was there. He searched the area for Lila's car but did not find it. He concluded she either had not been there or had been there and left safely. He decided to leave and search elsewhere for Lila and found his way back to the middle of the street and to his car.

Jason looked at the newspaper ads that he was using as a guide to search for Lila and one ad caused his heartbeat to quicken. It indicated she may have gone to look at condominiums situated on a bayou and, remembering what the young boy had said, if it had overflowed Lila could be in serious trouble in her small car. He started his car and headed for the Bayou Condominiums. When he arrived there the area was almost completely under water and many people were attempting to wade in to their homes. There had obviously been serious damage done to some of the property and Jason watched compassionately as the people attempted to save some of their personal belongings.

"Have they pulled that car out of the bayou yet?" he heard someone ask.

"Not yet," was the quick reply.

He rushed over to where two men were standing surveying the bayou that had overflowed. "What happened here?" he asked, afraid of the answer he might receive.

"Somebody lost control of their car during the heavy rain," one of the men answered, "and went into the bayou."

"What kind of car was it?" Jason asked.

"We're not sure but someone did say it was one of those little sports cars."

Jason's body stiffened with fear. "What color was it?" he insisted.

"I don't know," one of the men answered, "but

Charles saw it when it went in. Ask him." He pointed to a man wearing a red shirt and standing waist deep in water helping people as they waded through the deep water. Jason quickly waded out to the man. It was dark now and the rain had begun to fall heavily again. Charles held a large flashlight in his hand lighting the way for people to move about. As Jason approached him he threw up a hand indicating he should not come any farther. Jason stopped and watched Charles who was looking beyond him. A couple of minutes elapsed before the man pointed in the distance to Jason's right. A black snake, about five inches in diameter and approximately four feet long was swimming toward a clump of bushes and grass. Jason looked around him and became aware of the dirty murky water full of all kinds of debris. Again his eyes sought Charles.

"He almost got you," the man said, "what can I do for you?"

Jason eyed the clump of bushes and grass before he spoke. "I'm looking for someone who may have come here earlier to look at a condominium. She was driving a yellow MG. Do you remember seeing her?"

"Nope, haven't seen anybody like that," the man said. A loud noise that sounded like a shot startled both of them.

"Got him," someone said and held the dead snake up for all to see.

"You can bet there are plenty more where that one came from," another voice said in the darkness. "We'd better get out of this water."

The incident had frightened the people who were

still in the water trying to save their valuables and they frantically moved toward safety. "Someone said you saw a car go in the bayou," Jason said hurriedly. "What kind was it?"

"A white Jaguar."

Relief flooded Jason's body as he turned to wade back to his car. "Thanks for your time," he called to Charles.

"Glad to be of help."

Back in his car, Jason checked his guide, the newspaper ads, again. It would be difficult to get to West Belt from where he was with the city streets in such terrible condition, but he was determined to look for Lila. As he drove along he saw a convenience store and decided to stop and call Aunt Katherine to see if perhaps Lila had managed to get home. He tried the number a couple of times before realizing the phone was out of order. He then decided to go by his home, in case she was there, before continuing his search all the way out in the southwest section of the city.

"Where's Lila?" Violet asked when he entered the house.

"She's not here?" Jason answered with a question.

"No," the child said and ran into the library where Daisy and Aunt Katherine were sitting. Jason followed her.

"No luck?" Aunt Katherine asked looking anxiously at her nephew.

"No," he answered, and sank wearily in the leather chair behind his desk. "I thought maybe she had made it back here by now."

"We haven't heard from her," Aunt Katherine

said, "and I don't understand why she hasn't called to let us know she's all right."

Jason looked at his aunt quizzically. "The phone is out of order," he said.

She returned his puzzled look. "The phone is fine," she informed him, "I've just made a couple of calls."

Disbelievingly, Jason lifted the receiver to his ear. "It seems we can make calls out," he said, "but we can't receive them. Have you heard from Aunt Margaret?" he asked dialing her number.

"No, and I'm so worried about her," Aunt Katherine said. "Her phone is still out of order, although I've reported it twice."

"Yes, it is," Jason said replacing the receiver back in its cradle and then picking it up again to call the telephone repair service. After reporting the two phones, he dialed the police station to report a missing person—Lila—but was informed many people had been stranded and unable to contact their friends and loved ones. He was asked to call back the next day about noon if he still had not found who he was looking for.

Jason leaned back in his chair despondently and stared into the distance. "I think you should change into some dry clothes and have your dinner," Aunt Katherine said to him.

"I'm going back out to look for Lila," he responded getting up from his chair.

"But there's nothing more you can do tonight."

"I have to look for her." Jason was adamant.

"Do you think she's hurt?" Daisy asked tearfully.

Jason gathered the two girls in his arms and kissed

them lightly on the forehead. "No," he said wiping tears from their eyes. "I don't think she's hurt. She probably just needs some help in getting home." He kissed them both again. "Don't worry," he continued, "go up to bed now and get some rest. When Lila comes home I'll be sure and tell her to come up and let you girls know she's all right." Their large brown eyes followed him as he walked toward the door.

"Do you promise, Uncle Jason?" they asked.

"I promise," he said smiling weakly and raising his right hand.

It was still raining when Jason headed his car southwest to West Belt. The process of reaching the area where Lila had gone to look for housing was slow and laborious. Accidents, probably caused by car brakes becoming wet and malfunctioning, were blocking several intersections and Jason was finally forced to take a street map from his glove compartment in order to find his way via alternate routes.

Many hours had passed since the first morning deluge, it was now 11 P.M., however, in most sections of the city the water had not yet begun to recede. When Jason reached Pineville Garden Condominiums the area was flooded and looked to be completely deserted. Nevertheless, he parked his car in a high spot and with a flashlight waded toward the sales office. He saw no sign of the MG, Lila or anyone else and so he went back to consult his guide once again. He drove to Memorial Drive around stalled cars and through high water. The area was more alive than the previous one and boats were still navigating some of the flooded side streets and intersections. People were standing in small groups talking and Jason left his car and walked over to one of the groups. He explained he was looking for a friend and described Lila and her car to them. They suggested he talk with Mike who had been helping motorists out of their flooded cars since late afternoon. Mike, in his boat, had just brought a couple with a small baby to safety when Jason waded out to talk to him.

"Yes, I remember seeing a young lady that would fit that description," he said in a slow southern drawl, "but she wasn't in a yellow MG. She was on top of a green sedan with a couple of other people." He pointed toward the car. "I picked them up in my boat and brought them right here where you're standing, several hours ago. She should be home by now."

"She's not." Jason said. "Take me to the car. I'll pay you for your time." His hands went quickly for his wallet.

"I'm not charging for anything," the man said. "I'm happy to help anybody who needs it. Hop in. What do you expect to find by going out to the car?"

"I don't know," Jason answered. Mike took him over to the green sedan and went around it until Jason agreed to be taken back to safety.

"There's a little yellow sports car over there," Mike said, "but I don't know what kind."

"Can you get me to it?" Jason asked.

"Sure."

When Jason saw parts of the MG peeking through the water he immediately climbed out of the boat, into water chest deep, and tried to get a look at the license plate. In his groping he pulled up a chocolate brown leather handbag. He pulled it open and Mike held a flashlight so that he could read the name on the driver's license—Lila Drake.

"It's hers," Jason said excitedly and climbed back into the boat. They headed for safety. "This handbag belongs to my friend. Which direction did she take when she got out of the boat?"

"I don't know," Mike answered.

"Thank you very much for your help." Jason went back to his car and drove east through high water, stalled cars and accidents. At certain points along the way he stopped in bars, nightclubs and restaurants filled to capacity with people. When he did not find her he decided to try and get to Aunt Margaret's condominium. He hoped to find the septuagenarian safe and his deepest wish was to find Lila with her.

He was relieved when he saw Aunt Margaret's block was not flooded, but he was concerned there seemed to be no electricity in the area. With his flashlight he found her door and knocked.

"Who's there?" she asked after several minutes.

"It's Jason, Aunt Margaret," he answered. He heard locks turn before the door swung open.

"Are you all right?" he asked entering the house and kissing her on the cheek. "It's awfully hot in here," he added.

"It's so good to see you, Jason," she said. "Our electricity failed about five o'clock and also the phone. It's been terrible."

"I know," he said. "So many people have been

flooded out of their homes and cars." He took her candle from her and placed it on the small desk in the living room, glad he had stopped himself from adding some people had even lost their lives. "I'm pleased you weren't caught in the flood in your car," he said instead.

"I had been shopping and had to come through some deep water," she replied, "but I made it all right."

"Good. Have you seen or heard from Lila anytime today?" he asked casually.

"No," Aunt Margaret answered, and a worried look settled on her face.

"She's stranded someplace," Jason said, "but I feel sure she's safe."

"Are you going to look for her?" Aunt Margaret asked.

"As soon as I get you to safety," he replied. "Pack a bag and I'll take you home with me. It's not good for you to remain here with no electricity."

"I appreciate this Jason," she said leaving the room. "How is your family?" she asked, pausing for a moment.

"Fine," he answered.

They got back to the Tobias house and Aunt Katherine met them at the door. "I thought I heard your car." She stood back for them to enter the house. "I'm so happy you're all right," she said to her friend. "Was your home damaged at all?"

"No," Aunt Margaret answered. "We lost our electricity, that's about all."

"I assume you haven't seen or heard from Lila," Aunt Katherine queried.

"No, I haven't." The women exchanged worried glances.

"You two get some rest," Jason said, "I'm going to look for Lila." He walked to the door and started out.

"I don't think you should go out again," his aunt said, "it's 3 A.M., Jason. Get some rest now and go back out later this morning to look for Lila."

"Yes." Aunt Margaret agreed. "You'll probably have better luck after you've rested."

"I have to go now," Jason said, going out of the door and closing it behind him. He sat in his car a few minutes before choosing the direction he should take to continue his search. He assumed Lila would probably try to find her way home via one of the major streets running east and west, that would lead her to Caroline Street, so he decided to search each one of them. He drove over to Westheimer Road determined to hunt for her all the way up to Fountain View Drive.

The rain had stopped and as Jason drove he could see that much of the water on the major thoroughfares had begun to recede. However, cars and other stalled motor vehicles were still blocking streets and intersections causing him to make several detours. The city seemed deserted now with the exception of a few stragglers walking the dark lonely streets. Most restaurants and other public establishments were closed, but Jason searched thoroughly the small number that remained open. He took his search to San Felipe and then to Richmond Road investigating them in the same systematic manner and just as he was about to give up his search he remembered he had not checked the hotels in the area. He went to each of them and finally he entered the Houston Oaks.

Chapter Nine

The Galleria Roof had been slowly emptying since early morning. Lila sat at a table resting her head in her hands thinking of the foolish behavior she had displayed yesterday. By leaving the comfort of the Tobias home during the flash flood watch she had flagrantly ignored the concern that those who loved and cared for her had shown for her welfare. There was no doubt in her mind she had caused the family unnecessary worry for it had not been imperative that she find a place to live immediately. Spending a few days longer than she had planned in Jason's house would not be disastrous. Stifling a yawn and regretting not being able to contact the family by phone during the night, she looked out of the window into the darkness. She glanced at her watch and realized that the sun would be rising in half an hour and decided to have a cup of the free coffee that the club was offering its overnight guests. She knew her walk home would be long and difficult and the coffee would be just the thing to get her started. She filled her cup from the urn sitting on a stand near the door, added cream and sugar and went back to her table to drink it. There was one thing she was grateful for and that was the kindness and generosity of the people that she had come in contact with during the flood.

Jason looked around the lobby as he walked to the desk to check the register for Lila's signature. Not finding it there he turned to leave the hotel just as several people were getting off an elevator. It occurred to him that some people had probably spent the night in the club atop the hotel and he quickly took the elevator up to the Galleria Roof. His eyes searched each table and the several groups of people clustered about the room—there was no Lila. Tired from his all night ordeal and impelled by the smell of fresh coffee he found a seat and ordered a cup. He had no more clues as to where Lila might have gone and again the feeling of dejection possessed him.

"How much is it?" he asked the waiter when he placed the hot coffee before him.

"It's free, sir," the waiter replied, "you may have as many cups as you like from the urn over by the door." Jason looked in the direction of the man's pointing hand and his eyes met and locked with those of Lila's. In shock, they froze for a minute before rushing into each other's arms. They clung together as if afraid if they relaxed their embrace one of them would surely suddenly disappear.

"Where have you been?" Jason demanded, burying his face deep in the hollow of her neck. "I've been looking for you since yesterday evening."

"Oh, Jason," she whispered and began to sob, "it was so silly of me to go out during a flash flood watch."

He stroked her head and neck gently. "Don't cry," he said softly and took her face in his hands. "Where did you spend the night?"

"Right here in this room," Lila murmured.

"I didn't see you when I came in a couple of minutes ago."

"I had gone to call Aunt Katherine and Aunt Margaret, but their phones are still out of order. Are they all right?" Her anxious eyes searched his face.

"They're fine," he answered. "I've been so worried about you, Lila," Jason said, looking deep into her eyes. He slowly brought her face to his and their lips met in a singeing penetrating kiss. Her arms tightened around him as his warm hands caressed her neck and back. "Lila, Lila," he whispered softly in her ear and their lips met again sending flames raging through their bodies.

"Excuse me, sir," a waiter said, tapping Jason on the shoulder. "We're closing the club now."

Slowly and reluctantly they broke their embrace and with others took the elevator down to the lobby.

Jason slipped his arm around Lila's waist guiding her out of the hotel and to his car. Her breath caught in her throat when she crawled into the seat and saw her handbag. "Where did you find it?" she asked opening the bag and pulling out her personal belongings. "What luck," she added, "everything is still here. How did you get it?"

Jason pulled into the flow of traffic that was beginning to congest the eastbound lanes. "I found it in the water next to your car," he said.

"But how did you know where to look for me there?"

"You left clues." He smiled and took her hand in his.

"How?" she asked puzzled.

"You marked the 'home section' of the paper in the library."

"Oh, yes," she said laughing softly. "I didn't want to take the paper with me because no one else had read it and so I marked the places I was interested in and wrote the addresses on a piece of paper. I'm so glad you found it," she continued. "I hope you didn't go to all of them."

"Almost," he said, giving her a sidelong glance.

"Sorry." She made a face and squeezed his hand. "But how did you find my car? Is it still under water?"

The morning was beginning to brighten as the sun peeked through the remaining clouds in the sky. Stalled cars were still obstructing the streets, however, and traffic had slowed to a crawl. "Your car was under water when I found it," Jason said, "and Mike, the man who rescued you in his boat, remem-

163

bered you and saw a little yellow sports car during his rescue missions. He took me to it and in my efforts to check the license plate I found your handbag."

"That's terrific. I'll have the car towed out of the street as soon as I can get to a working phone."

"I've already made arrangements to have it towed home," Jason said.

"Thank you, Jason." She looked surprised. "I'm sure I'll have to buy a new one," she added sighing deeply.

"You don't have to make that decision today," he replied. "You have plenty of time to decide what you'd like to do about a car."

"You're right." She looked out of the window at the traffic jam and water that still stood in some of the streets. "When will this all be cleared away and things back to normal?" she asked.

"By afternoon," Jason said, and he turned onto a side street that led them out of the traffic.

"That soon?"

"Sure. The city can't stop because of a little water," he said teasingly, and turned onto Caroline Street and then into his driveway. He released her hand which he had been holding intermittently during their drive and walked around the car to assist her out.

"Thank you so much, Jason," she said again, looking up into his face. "I'm sorry I've caused you and the family so much worry. I do hope everyone will forgive me for being so thoughtless yesterday."

"I'm glad I found you safe," he said and kissed her mouth lightly. "And don't worry about being forgiven," he added. "We love you, Lila. Your safety is all that matters to us."

His words made her heart skip a beat and for the first time in over twelve hours she wondered about his relationship with Nikki Jocksay. They entered the house through the back door and walked halfway through the kitchen before meeting Mrs. Cobine who was entering the room from the hall.

"Miss Lila," she said, rushing to embrace the young woman. "I'm so happy to see you." She stood back and looked at Lila. "You look wonderful, but I think you could use a good breakfast," she added smiling.

"You're right, Mrs. Cobine," Lila said. "I'm starving."

"Breakfast will be ready in just a few minutes. Welcome home, Miss Lila."

"Thank you," she replied, returning the housekeeper's warm smile.

"We must go up this very minute and let the girls know you're home," Jason informed her as they walked to the stairs.

"Let's not disturb their sleep," Lila said frowning.

"They made me promise I would let them know the very minute you arrived home. Please don't make me break my promise." His dark eyes were serious.

"All right," Lila agreed hesitantly.

"They love you very much," Jason said, leading the way up the stairs.

"I love them, too," Lila confessed. He looked at her knowingly as they walked down the hall to the girls' room. They knocked lightly a couple of times and within minutes the door swung open. The twins' faces lit up like Christmas trees when they saw her and they immediately smothered Lila with hugs and kisses.

"We've been so worried about you, Lila," Violet said. "On television they showed people wading in water, some boys swimming down the middle of a street, water covering cars and almost whole houses. We kept looking for you every time they showed the flood, but we never saw you. Where've you been?"

"It's a long story girls," Lila said, "and I promise to tell you all of it as soon as I wash up and have some breakfast."

"Are you just getting here?" Daisy demanded.

"Why, yes," Lila replied a little surprised at the child's tone of voice.

"Good," she said. "Uncle Jason promised to let us know the minute you got home. I thought maybe you had come home last night and he was just letting us know."

"I've been here only a few minutes," Lila said exchanging glances with Jason.

"I kept my promise," he said. "Now get dressed and meet us in the dinning room for breakfast in half an hour."

"All right," they said happily.

Jason and Lila walked down the hall a short distance. "I'm going to shower and change," he said. "Let the aunts know you're home."

"I will," Lila replied and made her way to the guest quarters. Her aunt was happy and relieved to see her and so was Aunt Katherine when she stopped by her rooms. She promised to tell them all about her ordeal at breakfast and went to her rooms to shower and change.

Again she thought of Jason's statement as she slipped into an orange cotton skirt and white T-shirt. The words, 'we love you, Lila,' had stuck in her mind and she couldn't get them out no matter how hard she tried. She knew Aunt Katherine and the twins loved her as much as she loved them. But she was not as certain of Jason's feelings. Although he had spent all night looking for her and seemed to be overjoyed when he had found her, she knew that was no basis for claiming his love. She decided he had used the words carelessly and once more pondered his relationship with Nikki Jocksay and his strange influence over Hunter. She slipped into a pair of white flat sandals and left her rooms for breakfast.

They were waiting for her when she entered the room. "We thought you had fallen asleep," Aunt Margaret said as she took her seat.

"I'm too hungry to sleep, Aunt Margaret," she replied.

Mrs. Cobine delighted everyone by bringing in plates of fresh fruit. "You and Jason both look exhausted," Aunt Margaret continued. "You should go straight to bed as soon as you've completed your breakfast."

"We will," they agreed eating hungrily.

"Tell us about the flood, Lila," Daisy said. "You promised to give us every detail."

"You girls are sure holding people to their promises today," Jason observed.

"I did promise you the details," Lila confessed, "and I'll give them to you right now."

Mrs. Cobine served the remainder of the breakfast which consisted of sauteed beef tips, omelettes, toast, milk and coffee while Lila related her long exhausting ordeal to them. Jason interwove his experiences with Lila's and their accounts of the previous day and night held the family spellbound. They were about to leave the table when they heard the telephone ring. They cheered that it was again working and waited for Mrs. Cobine to announce the caller. Several minutes elasped however, before the housekeeper entered the room.

"You have a telephone call, Mr. Tobias," she announced coldly.

"Please take the message," Jason said, puzzled at her cold tone. "I'll return their call later this afternoon."

"She insists she must speak to you now."

"Who is it?" Jason asked.

"Your co-worker," Mrs. Cobine answered.

Jason left the room and took his call. Within minutes he was back. "I have to go out," he said finishing his coffee.

"But Jason," his aunt objected, "you haven't slept in twenty-four hours. Surely," she stumbled over her next two words, "your colleague can wait until you've had some rest."

"It's an emergency, Aunt Katherine," he said and left them.

The older women's attention turned to Lila whose gaze was fixed on her empty plate. "Well, dear," Aunt Katherine said softly, "why don't you go up and get some rest now."

Lila smiled at her feebly. "All right," she said and

rose from the table and walked what seemed to be miles to her room. She slipped her nightie on and crawled into bed. Although she fought it, Jason, and his quickness to respond to Nikki's call, were very much on her mind. Her thoughts slowly went back to his kisses and embrace atop the Houston Oaks Hotel and she laughed audibly. She had been foolish to think he had at any time taken her seriously. His deep concern for her welfare, considering all he had gone through to find her, had been short-lived; for all Nikki had to do was call and he had gone to her without hesitation. She had been unwise to think for a moment his words, 'we love you, Lila,' had meant anything special to him. Lila realized she had to forget Jason. She drifted off to sleep and slept fitfully for several hours.

It was early evening when Lila woke and went downstairs. She found Aunt Margaret in the library reading the paper when she entered the room. "Did you rest well?" her aunt asked, looking up from her paper.

"Yes, thank you," Lila said, not wanting to burden her aunt with the truth.

"Good," Aunt Margaret replied. "I'm leaving for home shortly and now I can go with the peace of mind that you're all right."

Lila settled herself on the sofa next to her aunt. "Are you taking a taxi?" she asked.

"No. Katherine is lending me her car," she answered. "It's all so inconvenient since I'll have to bring it back tomorrow, but I am anxious to get home to see about my belongings."

169

"Oh, I'll drive you," Lila said, happy for a good reason to get out of the house. "That'll save you the trouble of having to come back tomorrow."

"That's a lovely idea," Aunt Margaret said. "But are you sure you feel up to it?"

"I'm fine," Lila reassured her. "Is Jason home yet?" she asked, avoiding her aunt's eyes.

"No, dear, he's not." Lila noted the sympathy in her aunt's voice and regretted having asked the question. "I'm ready when you are," Aunt Margaret informed her putting her paper aside.

The traffic was back to normal on most of the major streets and roads. Lila would not have believed these same roadways had been blocked with cars and water several hours earlier had she not seen and walked them herself. The city officials had acted quickly to reestablish order on the major thoroughfares; however, it would take some citizens months and even years to replace their losses.

Lila thought of how lucky the Tobias family, her aunt and she had been not to have suffered any major losses as she recalled scenes shown on the television news of homes that had been completely destroyed. She realized, after examining her MG that Jason had had towed home for her, that she would have to buy a new car, but that was minor compared to what some had lost.

They arrived at Aunt Margaret's home without incident. The electricity had been restored and so had the telephone service. Lila and Aunt Margaret made tea and were drinking it and talking in the living room when the doorbell interrupted them. A neighbor and friend, Thomas Walker, had come to see Aunt Margaret and he was invited in and introduced to Lila. He accepted a cup of tea and joined their discussion on the major topic of the day, the flood. The conversation changed, however, when Thomas informed Aunt Margaret he would be moving at the end of the week and his condominium would go up for sale. Lila's spirits lifted as she anxiously waited for the opportunity to find out more about it.

"Why are you moving?" Aunt Margaret asked, surprised at her friend's news. Lila realized this was a possible chance to leave Jason's house at once and she impatiently awaited his reply.

"I'm moving to the valley," he said sadly. "My son has finally convinced me to move closer to him."

"I see," Aunt Margaret said unhappily.

"You must promise me Margaret," he said, "that each time you and the others go to South Padre Island you'll come by to see me."

"We certainly will," Aunt Margaret promised. "We're going to miss you, Thomas," she added.

"I'll miss you, also," he replied.

"Mr. Walker," Lila said, a little embarrassed that the man's news had delighted her, "have you found a buyer for your condominium?"

"Not yet," he answered.

"Would you consider showing it to me?" she asked. "I'm looking for a place to buy."

"I'd love to," Thomas said. "Margaret, it would be wonderful to have your niece living so close to you," he added happily.

"Yes, it would be," she said and turned to look at

Lila directly. "Dear, are you sure you wouldn't like to live with the Tobiases a little longer?"

"I'm positive," Lila answered adamantly. "May I see the condominium now, Mr. Walker?" she asked.

"Why, yes." Thomas Walker got up from his seat and walked to the door. "Come with us, Margaret," he said. Lila and Aunt Margaret followed him through courtyards that were beautifully designed with a variety of evergreen shrubbery and bright colorful flowers. In one courtyard was a swimming pool with lounge chairs and tables with umbrellas. It was here that he led them up a short flight of steps and into his house. Lila fell in love with the place immediately. The brick wall in the living area was perfect for the brass clock she had admired in the antique shop at the beginning of summer as well as paintings and posters that she had in storage. The smaller of the two bedrooms she would use as a study which would leave the living and dining areas free from clutter. The kitchen was small but bright and sunny and the deep green carpet that covered the floor completely gave it a warm and cozy air.

"How much are you asking for it?" Lila asked. When Thomas told her she became even more excited. "I'll take it," she said.

"Now dear, don't you think you should take some time and think it over?" Aunt Margaret asked.

"No," Lila said, "I'm quite sure this is what I'd like to do."

"Think it over for a couple of days, young lady," Thomas said, taking his cue from Aunt Margaret, "and if you still feel the same way about the place, we'll make a deal."

"All right," Lila agreed. "But my decision will be the same in two days as it is today."

"We'll see," Thomas smiled.

They left him and went back to Aunt Margaret's condominium where they prepared a light supper of broiled fish and a vegetable salad. Lila knew her aunt was concerned about her hasty decision to buy Thomas Walker's condominium and braced herself for the inevitable questions when they sat down to eat. She had no way of knowing, however, that her very first question would throw her off balance. Her aunt smiled knowingly at her before she spoke. "Why are you so anxious to leave the Tobias house, Lila?" Her tone was gentle but commanding. Silence hung over them while Lila thought of a suitable answer for her aunt. Not wanting to admit the truth, she gave a practical reply.

"I've completed my work there, Aunt Margaret," she said. "According to our initial agreement it's time I move out." She wanted her aunt to accept her explanation and drop the subject.

"I understand the agreement that you made," she replied instead, "but I don't think Katherine or Jason would ask you to leave knowing you haven't found a suitable place to live. I think there's more to this desperation to move than you're admitting, Lila."

She allowed her eyes to meet her aunt's. "Yes, there is," she admitted, "but I don't care to discuss it."

"You should," her aunt persisted, "it will make you feel better."

Deciding to buy Thomas' condominium and mentally decorating it had made Lila so happy earlier. Now, this discussion was causing her to feel uneasy. She wished Aunt Margaret would forget about her reasons for moving out of the Tobias house and accept her decision without question. "I can't," Lila said adamantly.

"If you're in love with Jason," her aunt went on, "I think you should tell him."

Lila got up from the table and walked to the kitchen door. "Never," she said in a low hissing voice.

"Pride has slammed the door of happiness shut in many faces," Aunt Margaret said following her, "I don't want it to happen to you, Lila."

"I can assure you I'm capable of being happy without Jason," she told her aunt.

"I hope you're right."

Lila helped her aunt clear the table and wash the dishes. They talked very little while they worked, however, she kept thinking of their recent conversation. She was determined to build a happy life for herself without Jason and her first step would be to move out of his house. Lila was delighted she had finally found something she both liked and could afford; she would move immediately.

"Thanks for dinner," she said kissing her aunt's cheek tenderly, "I must get back now."

"You're welcome, dear and thank you for driving me home."

On her way home Lila's mind drifted back to the brick wall in Thomas' condominium. She decided to stop by the antique shop to see if the brass clock she had liked so much three months ago had been bought.

She searched the back room where she had last seen it and to her surprise and pleasure the clock was still there. After purchasing it, she became excited again at the prospect of decorating her new home and decided to look in other shops before going back to the Tobias house.

She browsed in several boutiques before coming to one that featured bath and bed linens. Lila bought several sets of beige, white and lavender towels and made note of some lovely bedding that she would buy later. She put her purchases in the trunk of the car and drove over to Teddy's to have an iced tea.

The small restaurant was practically empty when Lila went in and sat at a table by the window. She gazed out at the passersby as she sipped her tea and her thoughts strayed from Jason to Nikki and Hunter and then back to Jason again. She wished she could more easily control her thoughts and center them on her new project—moving, but it was difficult.

"Hello," Samuel Jones, the short stout gentleman from the Galleria Roof greeted her. "May I join you?"

"Why, yes," Lila said. "How are you?"

"Fine," he replied. "I trust you found your family and home safe and dry when you arrived."

"Yes, I did."

"My little mutt and house had been spared also," he said. "What time did you leave the club?"

"Not until this morning. It seems I'm one of those who had to spend the night."

"I understand many people did. Would you like something to go along with your tea?"

"No, thank you." He ordered a sandwich and a cup of coffee.

"What are you doing in this part of town?" he asked. "I thought you lived much farther east."

"Yes, I do," Lila answered. "I've been shopping in some of the stores in this area."

"For anything special?"

"Yes. I'm moving in a few days and I'm shopping for my new place."

"I see," Samuel said. "Where are you moving to?"

"This area," Lila announced proudly, "over on St. James."

"That's very close to me." Samuel replied. "We'll be neighbors."

"Oh, it'll be good to know somebody in the neighborhood," Lila said happily. "When I move, I'd like to have you over."

"I'd be honored. Incidentally, some friends and I are having a party Sunday afternoon, if you're not busy come by. We'd love to have you." He gave Lila his address and they walked out into the late evening together. "I have a culinary shop a couple of doors down," he added, "why don't you take a look at some of the items, you may find some things there that you need." Lila accepted his invitation and went to the shop that was bursting with enameled cookware, molds, casseroles, tureens, cake pans shaped like the state of Texas and other culinary delights. She bought the Texas cake pan and promised Samuel she would be back for other items later.

Lila left Samuel thinking that again "Lady Luck" had come to her rescue. Not only would she have a new home in a few days, but she would have a new set of friends. She didn't need Jason in order to build a happy life. Once more her future looked very bright.

Chapter Ten

Lila arrived home about dusk and found Aunt Katherine sitting on the patio. "Did Margaret find things to her satisfaction?" she asked, when Lila took the chair beside her.

"Yes, she did," Lila replied.

"That's good," Aunt Katherine said. "How were the streets and traffic, dear?" she asked as an afterthought.

"Oh, you'd be surprised, Aunt Katherine," Lila

said, "some areas of the city look as if the floods never occurred and the traffic of course is back to normal."

"I'm not surprised," the older woman replied matter-of-factly. "But some people did suffer serious losses and I do hope the government is generous in helping them to rebuild their lives."

"I'm sure it will do all it can," Lila said. "I have good news, Aunt Katherine," she added.

"What is it, dear?"

"I've found a condominium to buy." Aunt Katherine's expectant expression turned to disappointment and she turned from Lila and looked out into the approaching darkness. Lila went on speaking, however, with as much enthusiasm as she could muster. "It belongs to one of your friends who is moving to the valley to be near his son."

Aunt Katherine looked shocked and turned to Lila. "Is Thomas Walker moving?" she asked.

"Why, yes," Lila answered, realizing not only had she upset the older woman with the news she planned to move, but also with the news of Thomas Walker's plans. "I'm sorry," Lila said, stumbling over her words. "If I had known our plans would disturb you so much, I would have been more tactful."

"It's all right, dear," Aunt Katherine reassured her. "I guess nothing ever remains the same no matter how perfect it may seem. When is Thomas moving?"

"The end of the week."

179

"And when do you plan to move?"

"Hopefully by the end of the following week."

Aunt Katherine rose from her chair and walked over to an old oak tree and leaned against it. "I suppose your mind is made up and no one can convince you that you're making a terrible mistake."

Lila avoided the older woman's gaze. Why was everyone so convinced that she was making a mistake? she sighed. Perhaps if they knew her reason for leaving they would be more understanding. But how could she tell Aunt Katherine or her Aunt Margaret that she loved Jason but she doubted the feeling was mutual. How could she stay in the same house with him, knowing that eventually their fervored kisses and caresses soon would not be enough. As it was, Jason need only look at her with his passion-glazed eyes and she was lost. She knew that eventually she would deny him nothing. Regardless of his relationship with Nikki and his hold on Hunter. But she would never be certain if it was love that flamed between them or simply physical desire. And Lila knew she desperately wanted his love, not a temporary affair that would leave her devastated.

"I'm moving, Aunt Katherine," she said firmly.

"When will you tell Jason?"

"As soon as he gets home."

"Jason is home," Aunt Katherine said, coming back to her chair. "He came in about two hours ago and had a light supper and went to bed. He's exhausted, Lila," she added.

"Then I'll have to tell him first thing in the morning."

"Yes." Aunt Katherine's sadness was reflected in her voice and she sat quietly for a moment as if struggling to find just the right words to say. "Jason isn't an easy man to understand, Lila. He's been so wrapped up in his practice and the girls that sometimes he's pulled in so many different directions he can't see the forest for the trees, as the saying goes." Aunt Katherine smiled, then looked at Lila gravely. "Jason may not say what you want to hear or act the way we might want him to. But he's a wonderful man and the woman who is understanding and patient will have enough love for a lifetime."

Lila left her sitting on the patio and went up to her rooms. She took out her luggage and began packing. She was annoyed that both aunts had been upset she had finally found some place to live. It seemed they were more concerned with Jason's reaction to her moving than in sharing her moment of joy. Tears filled her eyes as she placed her belongings in the suitcases. She felt alone. No one was supporting her decision. Lila realized, however, she had to do what was best for her happiness. The aunts would just have to try to understand her feelings.

Whispers and soft giggles made Lila look toward the door which she had left ajar. The twins, on hands and knees peeking at her, caused her to laugh softly. "I see you," she said turning from her packing. "Come in."

"We wanted to scare you," Daisy said as they strolled into her rooms, "but we couldn't stop laughing. What's this?" she asked, picking up the cake pan.

"A cake pan shaped like the state of Texas."

"Oh, it's cute," Violet said, taking the pan from her sister's hands, "are you going to bake a Texas cake, Lila?"

"Yes," Lila answered, feeling better now that the twins were with her. "Maybe I'll bake one tomorrow and get you girls to help me." She resumed her packing absently.

"That'll be fun," the girls said watching her.

"What are you doing?" Daisy asked.

"Packing." Lila replied, realizing she had begun placing articles in her suitcases again. The startled looks on the girls' faces caused her to stop her packing and sit on the side of the bed. "I've found a lovely little condominium to buy that's close to where my Aunt Margaret lives," she said. "I'm moving in two weeks."

Deep frowns wrinkled the twins' brows. "But Lila," Daisy said, "I thought you promised to live here with us."

"I promised to consider living here," Lila said, "and I did. However, after thinking about it awhile, I decided it would be best for all concerned if I moved into my own place."

"You don't love us?" Violet asked.

"Of course I love you," Lila said, and took the girls' hands in hers. "It's just that I need to live by myself for awhile."

"Does Aunt Katherine know?" they asked.

"Yes," Lila answered. "I've told both Aunt Katherine and Aunt Margaret."

"What did they say?"

"Well, they don't think it's a very good idea," Lila said, hating to admit the truth to the girls, "but I think they'll soon realize I've made the best choice."

"What about Uncle Jason?" Violet asked. "What did he say?"

"I haven't told him yet. Don't look so unhappy," Lila continued hurriedly, "I'll come to visit you and you can come to visit me. We'll see each other often."

"It's not the same as living together," Violet said.

"No, it's not," Lila admitted, "but I think it'll turn out to be just as much fun." The little girls sighed deeply and looked at Lila worriedly. She was sorry she had made them so unhappy, but she realized they had to be told. They would have to accept her decision along with everyone else.

"It's our bed time," Daisy said after a brief silence, "we'll see you in the morning, Lila."

"And don't forget about the cake," Violet added. Lila was a little puzzled at the girls' abrupt departure; however, she kissed them both and walked them to the door. After watching them enter their rooms, she went back to her packing.

She had completed filling one suitcase and was placing it in the closet when the door to her rooms swung open. Jason, in silk pearl gray pajama bottoms stood just inside her rooms. His hands hung to his sides in tight fists. His dark hairy chest heaved rapidly from his heavy breathing and his large brown eyes—bloodshot and glassy from lack of sleep—angrily searched her rooms. He pulled his lips into a straight taut line which barely allowed his low bitter voice to escape his clenched teeth.

"What are you doing?" he demanded.

Lila was taken aback by Jason's rude and sudden entrance and slowly anger began to creep through her body. "What do you mean?" she asked, attempting to keep her temper under control.

"The twins have just told me you're packing to leave. Is it true?"

"Yes, it is, Jason," Lila said flatly, realizing now why the girls had left so abruptly earlier. "I'm moving in two weeks." She walked to the windows and looked out and for some reason her eyes fastened onto the lounge chair by the pool where Jason had been affectionate to her so long ago. The memory of that early morning caused her heartbeat to quicken and the anger that she had initially felt for this irate man standing before her gradually melted away. She turned and met met Jason's gaze and for a moment forgot why he was there. "It's best for all of us," she said softly.

"Not all of us, Lila," he said taking her by the shoulders and drawing her into her arms. His lips that had been so tight and angry just minutes ago were now soft and warm as they pressed passionately against hers. Lila pulled away from him a little dazed by his kiss.

"How is Nikki Jocksay?" she asked icily.

Jason's eyes grew angry again as they searched Lila's face. "I find it very strange that you should think of Nikki at such a private moment," he said, obviously controlling his anger.

"I find it even stranger that you would create this private moment," she mocked, "after being with Nikki all day." Her anger had ignited.

His lips pulled into a derisive smile as he allowed his hands to fall from her shoulders. "I spent all night looking for you, Lila," he said. "Doesn't that tell you something?"

"Yes, it does," she replied, her lips curling to return his insult, "it tells me a lot, however, your spending the day with Nikki afterward tells me even more."

Jason turned away from her and walked to the bed and sat down. He leaned forward resting his head in his hands. "I haven't slept in almost forty-eight hours," he said. "I'm too tired to fight, Lila." He looked up at her and their eyes locked. "I love you," he said simply. "I looked for you the night of the storm because I couldn't have gone on living if something had happened to you." He held her gaze as she walked over and knelt down in front of him. He took her face in his hands and looked into her eyes. "I love you," he repeated, and their lips meshed in a long burning kiss. Jason slid to the floor beside her and his large warm hands caressed her face and neck tenderly. "I think I've loved you since the first time I saw you," he said softly against her ear.

"Jason," she said, catching his hands and stopping the assault of fiery tingles he was sending over her skin, "I must know what your relationship is with Nikki."

He smiled at her warmly and pressed her head against his chest. "Nikki and I are only co-workers," he said holding her close against him. "She has wanted our relationship to develop into something more now for some time but I have always viewed her only as a friend and nothing more."

"She followed you to Cancun and you went to her when she called today."

"She followed us to Cancun to try to prevent anything from developing between us," he said. "I realize my thoughtlessness while she was there gave you reason to believe I preferred her company to yours, but that simply was not true."

"And today?" Lila asked.

"Today *was* an emergency. A position in a California hospital finally came through for Nikki and we had some last minute work that had to be completed. She's leaving for San Francisco in two days."

"I see," Lila said pulling away from him in order to search his face.

"You're wondering about Hunter," he said as if reading her thoughts. "I can only tell you that Nikki and I have been counseling Hunter and his wife since a few days after Nikki's birthday party. For reasons that I can't disclose, it's best that he sever his relationship with you."

"He and his wife will be all right, won't they?" Lila asked, concerned about her dear friend.

"I'll do all I can to help them," Jason replied, "but they'll have to remain in therapy for a while."

She relaxed against his chest and tightened her embrace and he stroked her head gently. "I want you to stay here and be my wife, Lila," he said.

His words startled her and for a moment she had difficulty finding her voice. "Oh, Jason!" Her eyes filled with happy tears as she looked into his face, "I love you and yes, I'll be your wife."

"I've waited so long to hear you say those words," he whispered taking her face in his hands.

"I love you," she said again and this time their long and passionate kiss was punctuated with whispered endearments.

Reluctantly, Jason got to his feet and helped her up. Arm in arm they walked to the door. "I think we should let everyone know we'll be married soon," he said walking out into the hall, "I don't want two little girls crawling into my bed again tonight crying because they think you're leaving." He cupped his hands around his mouth and at the top of his voice made the announcement to the household. "To whom it may concern," he said, "Lila and I will be married soon." Smiling mischievously, he leaned against the banister and waited. Within minutes the twins, Aunt Katherine and Mr. and Mrs. Cobine were in the hall all talking at once.

"We must toast the happy couple," Mrs. Cobine finally said. "I'll chill a bottle of champagne."

"One glass of champagne, then I'm afraid you'll have to continue the celebration without me," Jason said, going over to Lila and kissing her lightly on the lips, "I'm tired and have to get some rest." They all hugged and kissed Lila again as tears of joy flowed from her eyes. She now knew that she had been wrong about this strong and wonderful man and that her life with him would be nothing less than happy and secure.

IT'S YOUR OWN SPECIAL TIME

Contemporary romances for today's women.
Each month, six very special love stories will be yours
from SILHOUETTE. Look for them wherever books are sold
or order now from the coupon below.

$1.50 each

$1.75 each

- -

SILHOUETTE BOOKS, Department SB/1
1230 Avenue of the Americas
New York, NY 10020

Please send me the books I have checked above. I am enclosing
$_____ (please add 50¢ to cover postage and handling. NYS and
NYC residents please add appropriate sales tax). Send check or
money order—no cash or C.O.D.'s please. Allow six weeks for delivery.

NAME_____

ADDRESS_____

CITY_____STATE/ZIP_____

Silhouette Romance

15-Day Free Trial Offer
6 Silhouette Romances

6 Silhouette Romances, free for 15 days! We'll send you 6 new Silhouette Romances to keep for 15 days, absolutely free! If you decide not to keep them, send them back to us. You pay nothing.

Free Home Delivery. But if you enjoy them as much as we think you will, keep them by paying the invoice enclosed with your free trial shipment. We'll pay all shipping and handling charges. You get the convenience of Home Delivery and we pay the postage and handling charge each month.

Don't miss a copy. The Silhouette Book Club is the way to make sure you'll be able to receive every new romance we publish before they're sold out. There is no minimum number of books to buy and you can cancel at any time.

This offer expires March 31, 1982